Sign up for our newsletter to hear
about new and upcoming releases.

www.ylva-publishing.com

Falling into Place

Sheryn Munir

Dedication

For those in their little corners of the world who
quietly push the boundaries from within.

Acknowledgements

CK, ML, LM, SR, and PD, for being my cheerleaders—you know who you are.

Pin, my Goodreads friend, for providing initial feedback.

Lee, for poking holes in early drafts and helping to hammer *Falling into Place* into a better story.

Astrid and Daniela, for saying yes! And for tapas, pizza, and great conversation in Leipzig.

Note

While most of the places mentioned in this book do exist and the historical events referred to really happened, plenty of things in and around these places and events have been fictionalized. Thus, any attempt to look for historical accuracy will be futile.

Chapter 1

FORGET CATS AND DOGS—THIS WAS the stuff of elephants and hippos. The rain was coming down in sheets now, much faster than the drains could siphon off to mysterious depths. Sameen huddled under the bus stop shelter, cursing her luck for having worn her new white churidar today; the dress's lower half looked neither new nor white any more. She knew from her previous monsoons in Delhi that the drains would soon pack it in and the water level would start to rise. She hoped she would be home by then.

She stabbed at her phone, but the Uber app remained as stuck as it had been fifteen minutes ago. It was still showing no available taxis, not even a damned pool. She was considering rebooting the phone—again—when it vibrated in her hand and she nearly dropped it in alarm. It was Rohan.

"Have you got a cab yet?"

"No, yaar. And it's still pouring here."

"Ah, damn it."

"I'll be there soon, Ro. Gotta go now. My battery's dying."

Poor Rohan—it was his birthday, after all. But her low-battery warning had been on for a while.

Stupid not to charge it in the office, Sameen thought. But she had been so caught up with checking the final proofs of that much-anticipated Loveleen Bing book and tussling with the cover designer on some teeny changes that would make all the difference, that she had completely forgotten. This book could make her career—which Sameen was acutely conscious of— and it had to be perfect. In fact, she'd become a bit obsessed about it.

Sameen gave herself a mental slap. What was wrong with her? It was almost nine o'clock, her boyfriend's birthday party was on, it was pouring with rain, no autorickshaws were around, and her cab apps had all simultaneously revolted. And here she was, daydreaming about some stupid book, Loveleen Bing or no Loveleen Bing. That said, even if she did manage to get a cab, she doubted she'd get anywhere soon—the traffic had barely moved in the last quarter hour.

Take that white WagonR, 1708—she'd noticed the number because it was today's date, 17 August. When she'd splashed her way out of her office and taken shelter here, it had been a couple of metres short of the bus stop. Now, it had advanced and was parallel to the bus stop. Bus number 413 had been standing at the T-junction to Sameen's left, gridlocked by the stream of cars turning at the light. From what Sameen could see, the bus was packed, but if she managed to squeeze herself in, she would at least be going homewards.

I'm not reaching home today, she groaned. She wondered if any of their friends heading towards Rohan's party would be passing this way.

As she waited for her phone to restart, she turned her attention back to cab 1708 and watched—with mounting resentment—the woman inside. She was typing away on her laptop. She had headphones on too, and if Sameen wasn't mistaken, she was talking to someone. The light from the screen bathed her face in white-blue light. The woman brushed a strand of hair from her face and frowned in concentration as she nodded and typed. Sameen leaned forward.

Wasn't that...?

There was a cacophony of horns and a flurry of movement as some secret signal hailed the possibility of progress for the traffic. No time to think. Sameen launched herself off the footpath and ran. Horns blared and tyres screeched, but she paid them no heed. She wrenched open the door of cab 1708 and hurled herself inside.

"What the fuck!" Tara screamed.

"*O teri!*" the driver yelled. He braked, but since the car was hardly moving, it didn't really make much difference. The traffic seemed to have stalled again. He switched on the light inside the car.

Tara stared dumbfounded at the drenched woman by her side, who looked just as shocked as she felt. Tara's handbag was open by her feet and she knew she had a can of deodorant in it. She reached in and thumbed the cap off, readying herself to spray the hell out of this creature. She was *not* going to be mugged on a crowded main road.

Then the intruder started talking.

"I'm so sorry! I didn't mean to frighten you. Sorry, Driver-ji. It's just that, it's raining so hard and I haven't been able to get any transport and I saw you—we've met at the Safal store in Malviya Nagar, don't you remember? The one opposite the bank? Remember, the other day we both wanted a pack of frozen peas and there was only one left and you said I could have it?

I'm really sorry about this, but I saw you and I was desperate and the traffic started moving, and there was nothing else to do but jump into the cab before I could explain anything. I'm so sorry. God, this is so embarrassing, but I would really, really appreciate it if you gave me a lift."

Tara's mouth fell open. She let the can of deodorant drop back inside her bag, relieved she hadn't maced this idiot. She did remember the frozen peas, and she was almost sure she'd seen this crazy fool around. She breathed and gestured to Prem that it was okay. "It's fine. She lives near my house."

"I'm so sorry," the stranger said contritely.

"It's…fine." The hammering in her chest was starting to abate. For some reason, the traffic had started to move again. "Where do you want to be dropped off?"

"Anywhere will do." She rummaged in her bag and produced her wallet. For a moment, Tara thought she was going to offer her money, but she only took out a card and handed it to her. "This was very rude of me, I know. Here's my card. My name is Sameen Siddiqi. I work in a publishing house. Oh, and here's something that can prove I'm who I say I am and not some random con artist." She produced a voter's ID that she thrust at Tara.

Tara took the card but waved away the ID. In any case, Prem had turned off the interior light and it was too dark to make out details. "It's okay, I remember you. But you did give me a heart attack."

"Sorry."

"My name is Tara Dixit."

They shook hands. "What do you do, Tara?"

"I'm a journalist."

"Oh nice. Must be an interesting job, producing what the rest of the world sees as news."

"Yeah, it's fun."

"What's your opinion about the Syrian refugee crisis? It's really heartbreaking, isn't it, all those people, having to flee? Imagine having to run away, leaving everything you have ever known, your home, your friends, your money, your things. It's quite disgusting, though, isn't it, all these world leaders and even news channels calling them migrants? Disgusting."

"Disgusting," Tara agreed, though she wasn't sure what was wrong about news channels calling them migrants. She needn't have worried about adding intelligent content to the conversation, because Sameen Siddiqi was quite capable of doing all the talking.

"Al Jazeera is the only channel I have some respect for," she went on. "It is the only one making a distinction."

Tara decided to tune out as Sameen launched into the politics of refugees versus migrants. Whatever invisible barrier had held up the traffic seemed to have lifted and, within twenty minutes, Prem was turning into Malviya Nagar. Sameen asked to be dropped off at one corner, and, following another round of profuse apologies and thanks, she disappeared down a dark lane.

Tara leaned back into her seat and sighed in relief.

Chapter 2

TARA'S ALREADY IFFY MOOD TOOK a further dive the moment she stepped into the house. The hum of the air conditioner welcomed her like a long-lost friend. Otherwise, apart from a rustle of paper, there was silence. Then her mother's voice came through, low and serious. Before Tara could call out, she spotted her through the open doorway

Tara's mother sat at their large dining table, papers and notebooks spread all around her. She cradled a phone between her head and shoulder, nodding, making notes on a scrap of paper before her, speaking every now and again.

"Hi, Mama," Tara called, forcing her voice to remain neutral. Her mother looked up and waved a distracted hello.

Tara dumped her things on the table in the hall and walked through into the living-cum-dining room. Annoyance seared through her. The room was a mess. Dirty dishes were stacked at the other end of the dining table to make space for her mother's latest project. The jigsaw puzzle Tara had started last evening—a complicated 1,000-piece one of a *Casablanca* film poster—had been unassembled and the pieces put back into their box. This incensed Tara anew. Even more than the pile of damp washing dumped on the sofa, clearly brought in hurriedly from the rain, or the empty, dirty glass and a half-eaten plate of snacks on the coffee table that had attracted a line of ants. Muddy slipper prints led in from the balcony. The window next to it had not been shut properly and had let the rain in—the sodden curtain hung limply and dripped on top of the wooden cabinet.

"Oh, Mama!" Tara said, running to close the window.

"Tara? You're back?"

"No, this is a ghost!"

Tara went to her room, wishing she could bang the door like a sixteen-year-old. After a quick shower, she changed with some relief into a pair of shorts and a T-shirt. When she came out, she noticed her computer was on. Moving the mouse to rouse it from sleep, Tara found a spreadsheet maximized on the screen. She didn't have to look too carefully to know what it was. Clenching her teeth, she quit the file and shut down the computer.

Yes, her mother had her crazy moments, but she was going too far this time. Really.

"Is there anything to eat?" Tara called as she went outside.

Her mother made an incomprehensible sound, busy organizing her papers in front of her into different piles.

The pressure cooker on the kitchen counter was still warm, which Tara took to be a good sign. A blue-checked cloth peeping out from a casserole was even better news. Tara twisted the lid open—parathas would be too much to expect, she supposed. It was. There were just plain old chapatis in there. She wrestled with the pressure-cooker lid, fingers crossed for something interesting. But there was only rice inside.

She poked her head around the dining room door. "Mama, why have you made rice and chapatis but nothing to eat with them?"

"Hmm? Have I?"

Tara went back into the kitchen and, with a lot more violence than necessary, measured out some dal to cook. She shoved the bowl under the sink and let the water run over the pulses as she pulled out a clean pressure cooker and banged it down on the burner. She sliced onions and garlic viciously.

She was still seething by the time she had set the dal to cook. It wasn't like she expected her mother to wait on her hand and foot, but she was the one who insisted they didn't need a cook. And it *was* nine forty-five—she'd been out of the house for over twelve hours.

To make a point—though it was debatable her mother would even notice—Tara went out into the living room and started banging things around as she cleaned up. The phone rang—the landline. It was lying on the table, next to her mother, who answered.

"Hello? Oh, it's you. Yes, yes, I got the details. He seems perfect." She paused and glanced at Tara. "No, I haven't told her yet. She's just walked in." Another pause, followed by a laugh. "Yes, so true, so true."

Tara gritted her teeth. She wished her mother had picked a less annoying obsession this time. She wondered how long this one would last.

"Look who's back from the wars!"

A loud cheer went up. Sameen brushed sodden hair from her face and waved sheepishly at the modest crowd that was supposed to be the cavalry for Rohan's thirtieth-birthday bash. The lights had been dimmed and a homemade banner said, "Happy birthday Rohan! Welcome to the 30s!" There were also balloons and streamers. Their living room pulsed with the deep bass from Rohan's eclectic music collection. A large bowl of chips and a smaller bowl with a dip were being passed around, and everyone had a drink.

"Sameeeeen!" Milind weaved between the cushions set on the floor for people to sit on and came to give her a hug. "Yuck, you're wet. Are those leaves in your hair?"

"Yeah, I've had to walk home while you've been warm and dry and eating my food."

The table groaned under the weight of the goodies Rohan had slaved to produce. He'd cooked for days. That had been no real hardship since he just needed an excuse to hit the kitchen, but the fact that only five people had turned up out of the twelve expected was a bit of a dampener.

"Just give me a moment to get into some dry clothes." Sameen stopped to give Rohan a peck on the cheek before slipping into the bedroom.

He followed her in. "Sent your book off?" he asked, plopping down on the bed that took up most of the room. She squeezed past him to the cupboard to get out the dress she'd been wanting to wear for this party.

She could tell he was a bit resentful. She didn't really blame him. "It wasn't the book. I couldn't get any transport. I had to gatecrash someone's cab in the end."

"What?"

"I'll tell you later. You get back to your party."

"Huh, some party."

As if on cue, the lights went out. Loud groans came from the other room.

"Hang on, people," Rohan called. A pale blueish light came on as he switched on his phone screen. "Don't panic. There are some emergency lights somewhere. Ow, sorry, Sid, didn't see you there."

By the time Sameen emerged, washed and as suitably dressed and coiffed as she could manage by candlelight, Rohan had managed to get some lights going. His laptop had taken over music duties, and people had started to drift towards the food.

Despite everything, the night was an unexpected success. There were chips and dips and sangria. There was music and dancing, and when the battery on Rohan's computer ran out, there was singing. The emergency lights gave out after a couple of hours and they sat around guttering candles, teasing Rohan about being over the hill and Sameen about hijacking cabs. Fortunately, the evening was quite cool, rare for August, so the absent electricity didn't seem to bother anyone that much.

Nobody showed any particular inclination to go home, and when things died down towards the early hours of the morning, everyone found sheets, pillows, and corners to stretch out in.

When the house was quiet again, Sameen leaned back in Rohan's arms and asked, "So how does thirty feel?"

He tilted his head as if he was thinking about it. "A little depressing, but I think it's going to be all right."

"Good to know. After all, I'll be joining you there soon."

"Mm-hmm," he said, his voice thick with sleep. "I still can't believe you hijacked a cab."

She smacked his chest half-heartedly. "I didn't hijack it." She closed her eyes. An image of Tara's face framed in the car window, the way the light from the computer screen etched shadows on her profile, flashed into her mind. She smiled. Actually, she *had* hijacked a cab. Sort of.

"Oh shit," Sameen said.

"Hmm?"

"I never even offered to pay for the cab."

But Rohan was already asleep.

Chapter 3

TARA RESISTED THE URGE TO shove the elbow-happy elderly gent into the crate of onions and forced herself to move sedately to the tomatoes section instead. She hated shopping at this time of the morning. She ended up jostling for space with a bunch of oddly aggressive seniors who hadn't seemed to have grasped the concept of lines or saying "Excuse me". Of course, she wouldn't be here at all if not for *another* not-quite-senior citizen—her mother—who had set out vegetable shopping but had come home with copious amounts of fruit instead.

Finding the counter empty, Tara rushed to have her stuff weighed and billed, wondering if her mother was actually, really losing her mind this time. She glanced at her watch to check if she was running late, then remembered it was her morning off. Maybe she would creep back into bed for another couple of hours. That was the best thing about her job—sometimes she didn't need to go into office till the afternoon.

"Tara?"

The first thing Tara noticed about the woman who had hailed her was her faded cotton drawstring skirt. It had a maroon-and-black zigzag design and was almost identical to one Tara had owned a good decade or so ago. Faded or not, this woman carried it off pretty well. Tara glanced up to lock eyes with her cab-napping acquaintance from last week, who seemed to be waiting for Tara to say something.

What *was* her name?

"Sameen," the woman offered brightly. "We shared a cab the other day, remember?"

Shared was one way of putting it. Tara smiled and said hello, abashed that she must have looked clueless.

"I must apologize," Sameen continued, "again. Not just for jumping into your taxi, but also, I completely forgot to pay you."

"That's no problem," Tara said, taking her change from the man behind the counter. "I didn't have to go out of my way or anything."

"No, but still. I must pay you. How much was the fare?"

"Really, it's not a problem."

"I insist!"

Tara looked around a little desperately. "My, er, office picks up the tab." A little white lie, but surely justifiable in the circumstances.

"Oh." Sameen, who had produced her wallet, appeared crestfallen. Then she brightened. "You must let me treat you to a coffee, then."

"Oh, but you don't have to."

"I want to! Are you free right now?"

"Er...I...um, how about tomorrow?"

Sameen peered at her for a second. "After work, then? Around seven? At that new coffee place next to Rimpy's?"

Tara realized there was no escape. "Sure."

But that afternoon in her office, she did fret about it to her best friend and colleague, Barkha.

"I'm telling you," Tara said, "I think she's stalking me."

Barkha looked her up and down. "Why?"

Tara put her hands on her hips. "What do you mean why? You don't think I'm stalk-able?"

"Don't be ridiculous. Why would anyone want to be stalk-able?"

"That's not what I said."

"You said, 'You don't think I'm stalk-able?'" Barkha leaned across Tara's desk to dip her hand into the packet of potato chips. She crunched noisily.

"That's because of how you looked at me and what you said."

"What did I say?"

"You said... Oho, stop it! You're derailing the conversation."

"You're boring me." Barkha picked the packet of chips out of Tara's hand and studied its contents. "You're obsessed with this woman."

"I'm *not*!"

Barkha looked up at the ceiling, popping a large chip into her mouth. "Then why do you think someone you've met twice is stalking you?"

"It's just that I get this really crazy vibe from her."

"Oh Tara, you wouldn't get a vibe if it came and sat in your lap," Barkha said with a dismissive wave. "Remember what happened that time when we dropped so many hints about—"

Tara snatched the bag of chips back and got up. "Get your own snacks."

"Nooo, don't go." Barkha got up to follow her. "Tell me more."

"No!"

"Pleeeease."

They went down the stairs, arguing all the way, and out to the narrow alley just round the corner where the tea stall was located. The makeshift structure consisted of a blue tarpaulin held up by thick bamboo sticks. The side of the office building made up the back of the stall, while the other three sides were open. One corner was occupied by a wobbly, run-down table whose front was an aluminium sheet with an ad for Pepsi on it. A large pan sat on the stove on the table, where Ramu, the proprietor, was making his special masala tea, which, according to Tara, was the best in the world. She took a deep breath, taking in the smell of ginger and cardamom. The table also held a few aluminium kettles, used and clean glasses, and a couple of trays strewn about. Two long wooden benches were placed in front of the stall, at right angles to the table.

Barkha plonked herself on one of the benches, which was unoccupied. An empty bench was a rare occurrence in this city of tea lovers. Tara ordered two glasses of masala tea, while Barkha lit up for a quick smoke.

"Okay, let's review the situation. Who jumps into a stranger's cab?" Tara said, trying to figure out which side of Barkha she should sit on to make sure the breeze wouldn't blow smoke on her face. It was always tricky, because if she sat too far away, the noise from the traffic, the hammering of the cobbler on his anvil, and the azan from the mosque—which was going to start any minute now—would make conversation impossible.

"You said she knew you lived close by."

"Still. Would you get in a stranger's cab?"

Barkha narrowed her eyes as she took a long, slow drag. "Well…"

"Don't answer that," Tara interjected, realizing something like that would be just up Barkha's alley. "Don't you think it's a bit creepy that she knew me? Then she turned up yesterday at the vegetable shop too."

The boy from the tea stall came over with their tiny glasses of tea. "No school today?" Tara asked him.

He grinned and shook his head. "Holiday."

She handed him a fifty-rupee note.

"To be fair," Barkha said as the boy counted out change, "she was trying to pay you for the ride. Which she should have done that day itself."

"But she chose not to. Maybe so she could seek me out later."

Barkha sighed. "You're quite convinced she's up to no good, right? Where did she say she worked?"

"Stone Apple Books."

Barkha drank down her piping-hot tea at top speed and stubbed her cigarette out. "Come on," she said and sped towards the office.

"Hey," Tara called out, looking alternately at Barkha's retreating back and the scalding glass of tea in her hand.

By the time she'd finished her tea and returned to her desk, there was no sign of Barkha. Since it was a slow day, she went down the corridor and into the large cubicle that comprised the HR department, and found her friend hunched over her computer. She looked up at Tara and beckoned her over.

"Look, I've found her—Sameen Siddiqi, commissioning editor, since 2013."

"I can see you are taking your assistant-HR-managerly duties very seriously."

Barkha switched to another tab. "And here's her Facebook page—who's that guy?"

Tara leaned forward, interested despite herself. "That must be the boyfriend whose birthday she said it was."

They spent a silent few minutes checking out Sameen's Facebook timeline.

"She looks pretty normal to me," Barkha said.

"Having a boyfriend and a job, and being a weirdo are not mutually exclusive," Tara reminded her.

"Okay, then, I give up." Barkha threw up her hands. "Congratulations, you have a stalker."

Tara rolled her eyes and went back to her desk, wondering what her next encounter with the crazy cab lady would bring.

Sameen opened the door to her house and walked in. The first thing she noticed was the new yellow tube light. She smiled. Rohan had replaced the harsh white light she hated with one of the "warm" light ones. She loved how it softened the edges of the room and turned the mishmash of furniture she and Rohan owned into one eclectic collection.

They were lucky to have landed this house. For Sameen it was definitely a step up from the poky little place she'd been in before. They even had an extra bedroom, albeit tiny, that Rohan could use as his workspace, and that balcony was great for parties.

The second thing she noticed was the delicious smell. She sniffed, intrigued, and called out, "Hey, I'm home."

"In the kitchen," Rohan said.

Of course. Where else would he be at this time of the day if he was home?

She dumped her bag on the sofa and went into the kitchen. Rohan was in front of the stove, dressed in a black T-shirt and jeans, attire that always made him look irresistible. He had his "decent" apron wrapped around his middle, the one that didn't have a rude message in Hindi on it. That meant he was cooking something exotic. She came closer and put her arms around his waist from behind.

"What's cooking?" she asked.

Rohan turned in Sameen's arms and planted a kiss on her lips. "It's a surprise."

"Won't you even give me a hint?" She tried looking over his shoulder at the pan on the burner.

"Nope." Rohan blocked her view. "Go freshen up while I make you a drink. What's it going to be today? Wine or whisky?"

"It feels like a whisky day."

"Right. Get out of here now." He gently shoved her towards the door and turned back to the stove.

Sameen blew a raspberry at him.

By the time she'd changed, Rohan had finished cooking and was sitting on the sofa with his gin and tonic, flipping through one of his architecture books. Sameen sat next to him, resting her head against his shoulder. She took a sip of the whisky he handed her and put the glass on the table.

"What did you do today, apart from cooking me a mysterious meal?" she asked. "And when are we going to eat?"

"Soon, greedy pig. I got a new job, by the way. The client wants me to create a mini Stonehenge in his sprawling garden in Gurgaon." Rohan shook his head. "I have the most bizarre job in the world."

"After your Japan stint, I'm sure you'll find better clients, and you can be well rid of the weird ones."

"Speaking of weirdos, how did it go with the cover designer?"

"Ugh." Sameen shuddered. "He refuses to make any changes regardless of whether it goes with the subject of the book. I spent the whole day negotiating with him. I swear, he has a pea-sized brain and a planet-sized ego. God, I'm so exhausted."

Rohan put his arm around her and gently squeezed. They sat in companionable silence for a few minutes, swigging their drinks.

This is the life, Sameen thought, feeling pleasantly drowsy. Idiot cover designers or not, she did love her job. And—no question about it—Rohan was the best boyfriend in the world.

Sameen was almost asleep when Rohan spoke. His voice seemed to be coming from a great distance. "Didn't get a chance to scare anyone in a cab today?"

She roused herself. "Ha ha. Very funny. Speaking of which, I met Tara, the woman whose cab I shared, at Safal this morning. I'm taking her to coffee tomorrow evening."

"Oh?"

"Yeah, I thought since I didn't pay my share of the taxi fare…"

"Wow. Not only are you a cab-napper, but you're also a freeloader. But then, I always knew that."

Sameen lazily swatted Rohan's chest with the back of her hand. "Shut up."

They lay curled up on the sofa, chatting. Finally, Rohan pushed her off, saying he was going to lay the table and serve dinner.

Sameen put her head back and listened to Norah Jones crooning in the background. She closed her eyes to soak in the soothing tones.

"Sameen, come. Dinner's ready." Rohan's voice pulled her out of the spell. She got up and went to the dinner table. Her eyes widened.

"What's that?" Sameen asked, pointing at the big bowl of thick brown soup with noodles and vegetables, garnished with diced peanuts.

"It's khao suey," Rohan replied as he served them. "It's a Burmese dish. I think you'll like it."

"This is delicious." Sameen dug into the bowl for more. "This is exactly what I needed today—an old-fashioned romantic evening at home. How did you know?"

"I have magical powers," said Rohan. "Now eat up, there's also dessert." He winked.

Chapter 4

SAMEEN REALIZED HER NEW FRIEND was a bit shy. Not that it bothered her. She could talk the hind leg off a donkey, so she could very well carry the conversation all by herself. And anyhow, she owed this woman for helping her out in her time of need.

"So what sort of journalist are you?" she asked, setting down a tray with two mugs of cappuccino and two slices of cake.

"I cover sport, mostly cricket and tennis."

"Wow," Sameen said. "I didn't know there were women covering sport."

"Of course there are."

"I know, I know," Sameen said, flustered. "That didn't come out right. I mean, I would imagine it's a bit of a boys' club. I heard about that ridiculous incident where that cricketer made a pass at a woman interviewer on live TV, and all these people defended him saying it's just a bit of fun. What an idiot."

"It's a boys' club all right. But it's not that bad if you know your stuff." Tara paused to tuck a strand of hair that had escaped her ponytail behind her ear. "Mostly."

Sameen laughed. "Yeah, I know what you mean. It's the same in all professions that are male dominated, I suppose."

"What about your work?" Tara fiddled with the silver ring on her thumb. She seemed somewhat restless, and Sameen wondered if she was usually like this or if she was bored out of her mind at the moment.

"Oh, publishing is full of women—not so much money, so mostly women."

Tara made a face. "It makes sense, though I wish it didn't. What exactly do you do?"

"I am a commissioning editor, which means I'm responsible for bringing in manuscripts for publication. We mostly do trade non-fiction."

"Oh, right, you guys did that book on corruption in cricket."

"That's right. But my department does the politics list. That night we, er, met, I had been working late, sending Loveleen Bing's new book off to press."

Tara's eyebrows went northwards. She'd been tapping her index finger noiselessly on the side of her mug, but her hand stilled. "*The* Loveleen Bing?"

Sameen groaned. "Yeah. She's a bitch, though. A complete diva. I hope I never have to work with her again. It has been a nightmare getting this book done and making sure we don't get sued for half the things she's said. She just wouldn't listen to anything we suggested." Sameen shuddered. "Ugh, let's not talk about her. She gave me nightmares, truly."

Tara smiled and drank her coffee. The tapping resumed. *Okay, so it's not me—she's naturally restless*, Sameen concluded with some relief.

"So you live alone?" Sameen asked.

"With my mother. You?"

Sheryn Munir

"With my boyfriend. We just moved into the house two, three months back. I like it here, better than my old place, which was such a weird house—one room after another, no passageway."

"Ah, those houses. There are quite a few of them here. But it is a nice locality."

"Actually", Sameen broke off a piece of cake, "the reason I was in such a hurry that night was because it was Rohan's birthday."

"Your boyfriend? Oh right, you mentioned the birthday. Did you reach the party on time?"

"More or less, though most of our guests didn't make it."

"It was quite terrible that night, all the waterlogging."

"Yeah."

Silence fell between them, though it didn't feel that awkward. Tara was contemplating her coffee mug, her thick, long eyelashes almost touching her cheeks as she blinked. She no longer seemed restless, and the calmness surrounding her drew Sameen in.

Tara looked up and their eyes met. Sameen quickly looked away, embarrassed that she'd been caught staring.

"What does Rohan do?" Tara asked.

"He's a landscape architect—he works freelance, so he's at home most of the time. He's a perfect homemaker, though, so it's great for me. I can barely even fold a towel straight."

"Lucky you," Tara said. "That night I came home to find that my mother had cooked rice and chapatis, but nothing to eat with them."

"Sounds like something I would do if I had to plan a meal. Have you lived in this area long?"

"Almost all my life." She was absently folding her napkin tinier and tinier now.

"Wow. I moved to Delhi only three years back. My parents are in Bangalore. I grew up there. But if you want to make it big in the publishing industry, you have to be either in Delhi or Bombay. I met Rohan the day I arrived in Delhi. It was like it was meant to be."

Tara smiled politely and unfolded her napkin. "So you've been together three years?"

"Not really. We were friends at first, and then we started dating. We only moved in together last year. But look at me, jabbering on. Tell me about you."

"There's nothing very exciting to tell. I've been working with the online sports portal Sportscene for the past five years. Before that I was with the *Hindustan Times*."

"And your family?"

"It's just my mother and me now."

"Oh." Sameen was not sure what else to say. She couldn't imagine what losing a parent must feel like. "I'm sorry."

"Thanks, it's okay." Tara pushed at cake crumbs with her fork.

Sameen decided it was time to change the subject. "So...do you get to go to all the cricket matches and stuff?"

Tara settled deeper in her chair, letting the fork fall back to the empty plate. "I do, now and again, though I don't always do live coverage. If you want tickets for the Twenty20 cricket match next week, I could get you some."

"Ooh, Rohan would *love* that."

"Great. I have a couple of passes to spare." Tara looked down at her hand and frowned at the napkin she was now shredding. She put it down and clasped her hands.

"Cool, thank you. And you know what? Early next month we'll be having a grand launch for Loveleen Bing's damn book.

You must come—it'll be super-fancy, five-star hotel, cocktails, and maybe even dinner."

"I don't know. Not sure it's my scene."

"I'll send you the invite and you can decide later if you want to come." Sameen took out her phone. "Give me your contact details."

Tara rattled off her number as Sameen typed it in and tapped the dial button. A musical tone sounded from Tara's pocket. "There, now you have my number too."

The conversation flowed easily as they finished their coffee and cake and moved on to comparing notes on the kind of films they liked, the books they read, and how it was getting progressively hotter every year. Sameen only noticed the time when her phone rang. It was Rohan calling to ask if she'd forgotten that they were going to Milind and Ashish's place for dinner.

She had and now they were late.

"I'd better get going," Sameen said, counting out the money for the bill.

"So should I," Tara said. "It was nice chatting, and thanks for the coffee."

"You're welcome. I had fun too." Sameen realized she meant it. "See you around?"

"Definitely." Tara smiled back at her.

Sameen walked home, trying to feel suitably guilty for forgetting about the dinner. But it was difficult, because she'd had a good time. She'd been expecting it to be nothing more than an obligation, a thank you for giving her a lift despite the, well, circumstances, but somehow she'd managed to lose track of time chatting with Tara. She was a weird bird, this Tara—sort of reserved, almost shy, but she had warmed up after a bit. Sameen wondered about her father—was it a recent loss? She froze mid-step. Tara hadn't actually said her father was *dead.* Had she?

Oh shit! thought Sameen. *What did I say? Did I say something stupid?*

An autorickshaw honked persistently behind her and Sameen stepped out of the way, absently heading towards home. Only when she reached the gate did she remember she'd forgotten to pick up the wine Rohan had asked her to.

Tara jumped when a hand appeared between her keyboard and computer screen. She blinked up at Barkha.

"Hello, still here?" Barkha gave a theatrical wave.

Tara rubbed her eyes. She hadn't looked away from her screen for two hours. "This stupid deadline."

"Yes, yes, I know, but deadlines will still be there long after you've ruined your eyes."

Tara stretched. "I heard of this app that reminds you to take breaks from your screen." She got up and crossed over to the next cubicle, where the printer was. It spewed out two pages, which she grabbed before coming back.

"You really need it," Barkha said. "Anyway, coming for lunch? Mike's birthday treat."

"Sure." Tara thrust the pages at her. "Proof this for me. I need fresh eyes."

Barkha made a face. "I'm not a proofreader."

"Oh, just do it."

"Fine, email it to me. You know I hate hard copies."

"Always some drama with you," Tara grumbled, reaching for her purse. "So where are we going for lunch?"

"No idea, but somewhere close by, so we're walking."

Tara's phone pinged as they followed the large office group outside. She glanced at it and groaned.

"What? Don't tell me you have to go back and write another story."

"Remember that crazy woman who jumped into my cab last month?"

"Oh right, the one you were convinced was stalking you?"

Tara ignored the jibe. "She's been at me to attend this book launch. Just sent me an invite."

"What sort of book launch? Will there be booze?"

"Sure to be. It's something fancy, at the Taj, this Friday. The launch of Loveleen Bing's autobiography."

"Whoa!" Barkha caught Tara's arm. "Loveleen Bing? I *love* her. We have to go!"

"We? No way."

"Pleeeease. It's at the Taj. The food there is amaaaazing."

"Didn't you go there just yesterday with Kunal?"

"The food is still amazing."

"Fine, you go. I'll forward the invite to you."

"Oh, come on. These things are no fun alone."

"Barkha, you know I hate this sort of thing. It'll be so la-di-da."

"So what? We can be la-di-da for an evening too. And anyway, Loveleen is so stunning. Come on, Tara."

"Take your husband."

"He hates hotel food." Which was funny because Kunal was in the restaurant business. "Please come."

"No."

Barkha opened her mouth to plead some more, but Tara's phone rang. The ringtone told her it was her mother.

She held up a warning finger at Barkha and answered. "Hello, Mama, what's up?"

"Nothing's up. I wanted to ask if palak paneer is okay for dinner."

"It's great." Tara's stomach growled at the thought of the rich, spinach-y taste, especially the way her mother made it. But her antenna went up. "Why?"

"What do you mean why? We have to eat, no?"

"Ri-ight. Okay."

Barkha raised her eyebrows.

Her mother cleared her throat. "Tara, listen, there's someone you must meet. It's your uncle's colleague's sister's nephew. His name is Prashant and he's the CEO of—"

"Mama, I'm not going to—"

"Just listen. I'm not asking you to marry him. Just meet him. He's a good boy."

"A good *boy*? You know child marriage is a crime, right?"

Barkha sniggered, catching on. Tara smacked her arm.

Her mother made an impatient sound. "Fine, *man*. A good man. He lives in the US. He's in town and he would love to meet you on Friday for dinner. It's the only day he's free."

"This Friday?" asked Tara, looking at Barkha.

"Yes. You said you had the day off on Friday, didn't you?"

"I do, but I have an important book launch to attend."

Barkha punched the air in triumph, making her dangly earrings dance.

Chapter 5

SAMEEN SHUFFLED HER CUE CARDS nervously and rubbed her clammy hands on her sides. She patted her hair and checked her blurry outline in the polished wooden door of the Durbar banquet hall. This was certainly not her first time moderating a discussion between highly opinionated people, but she'd never been in the limelight in this manner before. There were even going to be TV cameras.

Loveleen Bing, after all, was a household name, an international celebrity, some would say. The fact that Sameen had been able to persuade this renowned journalist to publish her much-anticipated autobiography with Stone Apple had greatly increased her stock among her colleagues, not to mention bosses.

This launch was a fancy do, organized by Bing's PR people. One of them came running down the hall and stopped when she saw Sameen.

"Sameen, ma'am, hello, all set? You know your cue, no?"

"Hi, Bindu. Yes, I'm good."

"Great. I'm going to start with the introductions in a minute."

Sameen knew that "a minute" meant nothing would happen for at least another ten or fifteen, and decided to go to the bathroom to check her hair and make-up one last time. When she got there, she discovered the loo was as five-star as the hotel—it actually had a sofa. Her hair and face checked—all good—she sat down to go through her points once again. But she was too restless to sit and decided to pace instead. The attendant looked at her curiously but didn't say anything.

The door swung open and two women came in, talking among themselves.

"Tara?"

Tara seemed momentarily confused. Then her face broke into a smile. "Oh, hi, Sameen."

"I'm so glad you came."

Tara introduced her companion, Barkha. They shook hands. "You're the cab, er, friend, right?" Barkha said. She had a naughty glint in her eye.

Sameen had the grace to look abashed. "So you know the story."

"Thanks for the invite. You even got this hermit," Barkha nodded in Tara's direction, "to dress up and come out. I usually have to drag her to these things. Now excuse me, I have to pee."

As Barkha stepped away towards the cubicles, Tara pointed at Sameen's cue cards. "Are you going to be speaking?"

Sameen made a face. "I have to moderate the panel."

"Wow. Are you nervous?"

"Are you kidding? I'm *dying*."

Tara smiled. "Well, if it makes you feel any better, you look stunning. That sari is beautiful. I love this colour."

"Really?" Sameen asked. "It's my mother's. Are you sure I don't look like an aunty?"

"You look nothing like an aunty."

"Phew."

Barkha came out of the bathroom, and she and Tara went on their way. The mic screeched, which meant things were getting under way. Sameen checked one last time that her sari wasn't going to trip her and hurried down the hall. The interlude with Tara and her friend had broken the tension.

Tara stifled a yawn and checked her watch. She crossed and then uncrossed her legs, and tapped her feet, trying to ignore the balding old man droning on behind the lectern. Her top felt a little tight around the armpits. She wondered if she had put on some weight. She hadn't been running regularly this year, after all. Her mobile vibrated. It was one of her aunts on the family WhatsApp group with a stupid joke that she probably didn't realize was highly offensive on multiple counts.

The CEO of Stone Apple Books continued his boring speech. Even Barkha seemed restless. The only saving grace so far had been the servers circulating with trays of drinks and snacks. Tara had armed herself with a glass of red wine and helped herself from every tray of mini quiches and bruschetta that passed her.

There was a smattering of applause as the CEO left the stage. The MC, a tall, thin woman—made even taller by her tottering heels, and thinner thanks to the tiny black dress she'd squeezed herself into—introduced Loveleen Bing with the usual rubbish about her needing no introduction.

"She looks incredible, doesn't she?" Barkha whispered.

Tara had to agree. Loveleen Bing definitely had presence and she knew how to dress to make it even larger. She came onstage to thunderous applause. She was a controversial figure, no doubt, but she did roam in exalted circles. She'd had the ear of the men and women who ran the country, and had never shied away from speaking her mind. She commanded importance and exuded authority. In the course of her career, she had had death threats, been almost stabbed and shot at, and once even abducted. Tara had never seen her in person before, but found her to be much more impressive than her photographs.

The MC went on to introduce the chief guest who would officially release the book and two others who were going to discuss its background. Finally, she introduced Sameen as the publisher and moderator of the panel.

After another speech, the book was unveiled. By the time the MC called the panel to the stage, Tara was on her third glass of wine and the servers were inexplicably not coming her way anymore. Sameen picked up the mic, but before she could speak, there was a screech of feedback.

She held the mic away from her face. "Everyone has an opinion these days."

The audience tittered, and Sameen waited for them to settle before she started on the funny story of how she had pursued Loveleen Bing until she had agreed to sign with Stone Apple. The panel was to discuss something to do with freedom of expression, and Tara was quite impressed at how Sameen steered the jokey banter between the speakers to a serious discussion on intolerance. Despite being the only relatively unknown person on the panel, she managed to hold her own, and the speakers followed her lead with good grace. The elegance with which she wore the shimmery silk sari—a huge contrast from her attire when they'd bumped into each other at the Safal store—only added to her air of authority.

Tara jumped when Barkha elbowed her. "Hmm, what?"

"You're not listening."

"Sorry, I was…"

"Yes, you were rapt in the discussion. Still bored, are we? Anyway, I was asking if they're going to serve dinner."

"Yeah…I don't know. Hush, I want to listen to this."

"Your ditzy friend is doing a great job."

"She is." A happy warmth filled Tara. It was probably the wine.

Chapter 6

SAMEEN SAT ON THE SOFA in the bathroom, letting out relief wash over her. Loveleen Bing and her entourage had left, all the big shots had gone, and the evening had been a resounding success. She leaned her head back and closed her eyes. She was worn out—public speaking did that to her. It started with a dose of nerves, followed by the high of the performance, and the feeling of having the life sucked out of her when it was over.

"Hello again," a voice said.

Sameen opened her eyes. "Oh, we must stop meeting like this," she said to Tara.

"Well, it's better than you jumping into my cab." Tara sat beside Sameen. "You were fantastic tonight. The way you handled those squabbling men was—" Tara put her thumb and forefinger together in an O of appreciation.

"Why, thank you."

"You're welcome. You look worn out, though."

"I am. I was thinking of running away quietly."

"Well, I was going to call for a taxi. Can I give you a lift?"

"I have an office car. It's my turn to give you a lift." Sameen jumped up and picked up her bag. "Come, let's run away together."

It was a nice September evening, and Sameen asked the driver to switch off the AC so they could keep the windows down.

"Where's your friend?" she asked Tara, who was squinting into the breeze, letting her hair blow backwards.

"She left—she had to go in the other direction. She said to say thank you—she had a great time."

"She's very welcome. And I should thank you, and also on behalf of Rohan, for the cricket passes. We had a great time too."

"Oh, any time."

The car stopped at a red light. Tara, whose hair had blown all over her face, tried to get it back in some sort of order. She seemed to have had a haircut. It was short, shorter than shoulder-length, cut in a way that the front was longer than the back, and it fell in a straight, silky sheet, framing her face. Sameen envied that sort of hair. Hers was wild and frizzy.

"I love your hair," she said. "Where do you get it done?"

"My mother does it."

"Really?"

"Yeah, she trained as a hairdresser and she uses me to practise on."

"Lucky you."

"Only when I get to choose my own hairstyle."

The light turned green and they started to move. Then the engine sputtered and died.

"What happened?" Sameen called out.

The driver, muttering under his breath, tried to start the car again, but it just wouldn't cooperate. Impatient horns sounded from behind them. The car started finally, but it coughed and went out again by the time they had crossed the traffic light. The driver managed to steer it to the edge of the road. Then he got out and went to examine things inside the bonnet.

"Uh-oh, this doesn't look good," Sameen said.

"It's not that far," Tara pointed out. "Want to walk home?"

Sameen looked at her feet doubtfully. Her heels had torn a strap that evening and she'd had to wear her backup shoes, which were quite flat. "It's your lucky day; I'm in my walking shoes."

"Come on, then."

"Driver-ji, we're going to walk from here," Sameen called to the driver, who was on the phone, yelling at someone.

He looked aghast. "But madam, I'm getting another car."

"It's all right, don't worry."

"But madam," he called again as Tara and Sameen started to cross the road. "Madam, come back, the car is coming!"

The road cleared and they ran across the street, giggling like errant schoolgirls.

"I feel a bit light-headed," Sameen confessed. "I don't remember how much wine I had."

"Me neither," Tara said. "Your boss was so boring, I had to drown my sorrows."

Sameen snorted with laughter.

A light drizzle started. Sameen didn't mind it, and it didn't seem to bother Tara at all, if her lazy smile was anything to go by. There was a wide enough footpath to walk abreast, and as they did, they started to talk. The wine had clearly let down Tara's walls, and she was much more garrulous than ever before.

"I have a confession to make," she said.

Sameen turned towards her. "Is it the kind that will make me an accomplice?"

Tara narrowed her eyes, as though pretending to think. Raindrops had settled on her head, making it seem like tiny diamonds were woven into her hair, which glittered as they moved in and out of the streetlights. "Definitely. If I go down, you're coming with me."

"All right, then, I guess I have no option but to take my chances."

"Well, the only reason I came tonight was because my mother was sending me on a blind date with some guy she hopes I'll marry."

For a moment Sameen was sure Tara was winding her up. Then she caught a glimpse of her serious face and burst out laughing. The next thing she knew, she had stumbled on a broken tile. The paper bag full of books she was carrying flew out of her arms and split open on the footpath before them.

Tara caught her arm. "Careful."

"I'm fine," Sameen said, still giggling. "You're joking, right? About the blind date?"

"No, I'm very serious," Tara replied, letting go of her arm. "You okay?"

"Yes, thanks." Sameen bent to pick up her books. Tara stooped to help. "So does your mother make a habit of sending you out to meet random guys, then?"

"My mother is a law unto herself. If I started telling you all she does, we're going to be here all night and then some."

"But a blind date." Sameen shook her head. "Sounds so…"

"American?"

Sameen burst out laughing again. She would never have guessed Tara could have such a caustic sense of humour. "So do you always manage to get out of them?"

"Nope," Tara said. "I've been on at least half a dozen, each more horrifying than the other."

"Do tell."

"Well, let's see." Tara handed Sameen her books. "There was this guy who parked next to my car and scraped it when he opened his door. We had a raging fight right there before we even knew we were meeting each other. Needless to say, it was a very stilted dinner."

"I'd have loved to have been a fly on the wall when you discovered you were each other's dates."

"Ha, that would have been entertaining. Then there was this other guy who gave very specific instructions to the server about what to put in his cocktail. He must have ordered about five of those drinks in the first half an hour, but he also kept excusing himself every ten minutes or so to go to the bathroom. I must say I really enjoyed that dinner because he spent most of that evening in there, leaving me to finish the delicious roast chicken he had decided we were going to share."

Sameen chuckled. "So not all bad experiences, then?"

"Well, there was ultra-conservative, right-wing guy who spent the first ten minutes ranting about how drinking and smoking were wrecking our culture. He wanted me to quit my job, produce at least two sons, cover my head, and become a vegetarian."

Sameen's mouth fell open. "How did you handle that?"

"Oh, easy. I ordered a beer and he walked out."

"Wow. I'm really glad to come to your rescue. Who knows what you might have had to fight off today."

"I had a really good time today," Tara said.

"And what about any future lover boys? What will you do the next time your mother wants you to meet someone, hmm?"

"Can't you have another book launch?"

Sameen placed her hand on Tara's shoulder briefly. "I'll see what I can do, my friend," she said gravely.

That made them giggle again.

Soon, they turned into a lane and Tara stopped at a gate. "Here's my stop. I didn't realize we'd walked so fast."

"This was fun," Sameen said. "Especially the walk. It's strange, but I don't feel so tired anymore."

"Yes, it was a nice night for a walk. I'm almost glad the car broke down."

"We've had some entertaining journeys, haven't we?"

"That we have," said Tara, unlatching the gate. She looked back at Sameen and smiled. "Goodnight, then."

"Night."

Sameen walked home with a light step, humming an old Bollywood song about a girl out in the rain at night. The book launch was a distant memory.

Tara:
Hi, Sameen, this is Tara. I accidentally went home with one of your books last night. Should I drop it at your place sometime?
-10:17 a.m.

Sameen:
Oh, so that's where it went. I'm so sick of it, want to tell you to throw it away!! Just joking! Can I pick it up after work tonight?
-10:20 a.m.

Tara:
Ok. Will call when I reach home.
-10:21 a.m.

Only when she was in her taxi on her way home that evening did Tara remember about the book. She called Sameen.

"Oh, hi, Tara," Sameen said breathlessly. "Are you home already?"

"I've just left my office. It should take me about forty-five minutes to be home."

"Cool. I'll leave here in about twenty or so."

"Listen, I should be passing your office in around twenty minutes to half an hour. Why don't I give you a lift?"

"That would be wonderful," Sameen said. "If you're sure it's not out of your way."

"Not at all. See you then, at the same bus stop?"

"Yep, see you."

Twenty-three minutes later, the car pulled up behind a large green bus. Sameen hopped down from the footpath and bent to the window. "May I please come in?" she asked, the picture of demureness.

Tara laughed. "Let me think about it."

The driver, Prem—the same one from that day—was looking aghast. "Madam! It's the same madam!"

"It's fine, Prem. She's not carrying her gun today," Tara said, still grinning as she unlocked the door. "Hop in."

"Hi," Sameen said, settling in. "Thanks for the lift. Again."

"You're welcome, again." Tara handed her the book. "And here's your precious autographed copy of Loveleen Bing's memoirs."

"Thanks, though if I hear that damned woman's name again, I'm going to kill myself."

"That bad?" asked Tara.

"Worse. She's made my life miserable, even almost made me miss my boyfriend's thirtieth birthday party, as you well know. Let's change the subject."

"So when do you usually leave work?" asked Tara.

"Around this time," said Sameen, "but it always takes me ages to find an autorickshaw or a taxi. I'm seriously thinking about getting myself a car. But then I'll probably be worrying about parking."

"That's true." Tara waved at the bumper-to-bumper traffic around them. "People seem to be buying cars like they're going out of fashion." They'd been at the same traffic light for the past ten minutes.

"So you don't have a car either?"

"My mother has one. She says I can borrow it whenever I want, but she always has these complicated plans and I rarely get to see the inside of it. I'm not complaining, though. I prefer being driven around by Prem."

Prem turned around and beamed at them. "You are my best customer, madam."

"That's because you're the only person in Delhi I know who understands the concept of lane driving, Prem."

"Maybe what I need then," Sameen said, "is not a new car but Prem's number."

"You'll have to prise it out of my cold, dead fingers."

Tara liked Sameen's laugh. The way she would shut her eyes, tilt her head back, and chuckle was quite charming. She was a bright woman who could seamlessly switch between being frivolous and sensible depending on what the situation demanded. Sameen could hold her own in any situation, and she definitely had a great sense of humour. Spending more time with her wouldn't be too unpleasant.

"I have a better idea," Tara said. "Since I pass your office on my way home almost every day, why don't we ride back together?"

"Sounds like a great idea, but don't journalists keep odd hours?"

"Only when I'm involved in live coverage, but most days I leave office at the same time. We could figure out a way to coordinate."

"And it won't be a detour for you?"

"Not at all," Tara said. "In fact, I'd be glad for the company part of the way."

"Also," Sameen added hesitantly, "er, I do feel a bit guilty imposing on your office taxi."

"Ah, that." Tara felt sheepish. "It's not exactly an office taxi. I have a running tab that I settle every month. I just said it that day to get rid of you."

"Oh!" Sameen struck a dramatic pose, hand on her chest. "I. Am. Hurt." Then she laughed. "Fantastic. That means we can share the fare too."

As they cruised towards Malviya Nagar Market, Sameen sighed at a tandoori chicken stall, where plump, marinated chickens turned slowly and tantalizingly on a spit. "I could eat a horse."

Tara followed her gaze. "I'm always famished at this time too," she admitted. Her mouth watered at the thought of sinking her teeth into a juicy chicken leg, maybe with some onions and mint chutney on the side.

"Hey, want to grab a bite?" Sameen cut into her delicious daydream. "Let's get off here and find something deep-fried to eat."

Tara turned towards her. "Are you serious?" What a fantastic idea. Why hadn't *she* ever considered it?

"Yes, absolutely! Driver-ji, please stop here."

And before she knew it, Tara found herself standing on the road, amidst the ear-splitting cacophony. This was why she avoided the market, especially in the evening. Cars and autorickshaws honked, people talked, laughed, argued, and temple bells pealed.

"Come on," Sameen yelled over the noise, and expertly dodged the traffic and the pedestrians as she snaked her way to the other side. Tara followed close behind.

The market was teeming with people. It was difficult to navigate without getting run over, if not by cars, then by the bicycles, scooters, and motorbikes. Tara hated that no footpaths were left anymore—they were all occupied by roadside stalls, or rather, what had started out as stalls but were now semi-permanent structures. Even the big shops, with their generous floor space, spilled out on to the footpaths. She glanced at an elaborate display of colourful plastic buckets and a variety of household items. When she was younger, she would accidentally on purpose kick these over.

They weaved their way between a row of scooters and motorcycles parked haphazardly in what was a pedestrians-only space, and stepped down into the main market through an opening in the low wall that separated the row of shops from the road. The smells from the eateries made Tara's mouth water. The hot, syrupy aroma of freshly made jalebis mixing with the spicy scents of samosas and kachoris being fried, and golgappas being doled out.

Her stomach growled as they passed a couple of young men selling momos from a table outside a grocer's shop.

"Hey, Sameen, momos...oh, chaat...or maybe bhelpuri..." Tara called out.

But it was too noisy for Sameen to hear her. In any case, she was busy disappearing down one of the side alleys of the market, zigzagging between the crowd, and it was all Tara could do to keep up. Despite her mere three years in the area compared to the lifetime Tara had lived there, Sameen was impressively well acquainted with the local food outlets.

Tara followed her into a narrow alley between a shop that sold baby clothes and one that had a variety of lurid stationery, and came out on the back lane of the main market. It was still crowded here, though not as much, and it was quieter. Sameen stopped in front of a tiny asbestos-roofed shack. It had a handful of chest-high tables around which customers stood, eating greasy snacks off paper plates.

"What is this place?" Tara asked. She couldn't recall the last time she'd explored the back lanes of the market. A bright green board with red-and-white lettering said "Sonu's Snack Centre—world-famous samosa, first-class jalebi."

"You like samosas?" Sameen asked, her eyes glinting.

"Who doesn't? And jalebis too, before you ask."

"Lovely!" She waved to an elderly man who was scribbling on a pad behind the counter. "Sonu Uncle, namaste. Two samosas and one plate of jalebi. Quickly, please."

Sonu "Uncle" sprang into action. He had one of his boys clear a table by unceremoniously shooing a pair of lingering customers out, and before Tara knew it, two gigantic samosas and a mound of hot, juicy jalebis appeared before them.

Tara picked up a large, glowing, orange jalebi, broke off a bit, and dropped the sticky sweet into her mouth. She closed her eyes. "Oh, divine. Sameen, you are a genius for finding this place."

"I know, right?" Sameen mumbled around the samosa she was devouring.

"You're so full of surprises," Tara said.

Sameen winked at her and said in an exaggerated accent. "You ain't seen nothing yet, babe."

Tara smiled at the mischievous twinkle in her eye. Befriending Sameen had to have been one of the best decisions she had made in her life, she thought, as she attacked her samosa with gusto.

Chapter 7

"You drive a hard bargain, Tara, but I can't do this anymore," Sameen said, shaking her head.

"Why not?" Tara demanded.

"It's not right."

Tara narrowed her eyes, but Sameen had turned away and was staring out of the window of Prem's taxi that was taking them home. It had been a couple of weeks since they had started travelling together, with Tara picking Sameen up on the way as planned.

"Come on. You have to give me a solid reason if you're going to ditch our evening snacking expeditions."

"Rohan is starting to get a bit suspicious about why I'm never hungry when I come home these days. He's a little miffed too, as he's taking some Japanese cooking lessons online."

"Pfft, Rohan," Tara said with a dismissive shake of her head. "You can't be scared of him."

Sameen laughed. "I'm not scared of him. I just feel bad. And all that junk food. Come on, Tara, it can't be good for us."

"That's the trouble with you young women these days," Tara grumbled, "letting their boyfriends control them." She glanced at Sameen through the corner of her eye, checking to see she knew she was joking.

"Haww." Sameen clapped her hand to her mouth, doing a decent imitation of a disapproving Delhi-ite. "Below the belt."

Tara grinned and moved in for the kill. "I guess this means I don't take you to the new snack joint that just opened in Saket." She raised an eyebrow, a slight smile playing on her lips as she watched the range of expressions passing across Sameen's face. "Maybe I'll see if Mama wants to come with me."

"Ah, damn it." Sameen thumped her fist into her hand. "That's not fair. You can't go there without me."

"But you just said you'd rather eat with Rohan," said Tara with an innocent air. "And that junk food will kill us."

"Oh, pish-posh. A bit of deep-fried goodies keeps the heart ticking."

"And what if Rohan finds out?"

"Screw Rohan. I'm coming with you and that's that."

"Hmm, I don't know. Maybe you have a point. Maybe we shouldn't do this anymore—" Tara said, stroking her chin.

"Tara Dixit, you stop this right now. Listen, I'll make you a deal. You take me to the new snack place today and I'll treat you to the best bhelpuri in all of Delhi. What do you say?"

Tara looked at the roof of the taxi and scratched the side of her neck, pretending to think it over. Then she grinned at Sameen and extended her hand.

"Deal."

Sameen, beaming, took Tara's hand and shook it firmly. "Deal."

Waiting at the same bus stop where she'd taken shelter from the rain almost two months ago, Sameen pondered how quickly she and Tara had become friends. Some people just click, she realized. Otherwise, jumping into a stranger's cab was more likely to land you an appointment with the cops than anything else.

Prem's white WagonR came to a stop by the footpath. Sameen opened the back door and got in.

"Hi," said Tara, handing her a plastic cup with a cover. "It's a little cold, I'm sorry."

Sameen took a sniff and the smell of tomato soup filled her nose. "Mm," she said after taking a sip. "It's good."

"I told you."

The other thing that had been unexpected was the way they'd bonded over food. She was kicked to see that her enthusiasm for food had rubbed off on Tara. "I never believed a vending-machine beverage could be so good."

"I know. So what's the plan for this evening?"

"Rohan's downloaded the new episode of *The Good Wife*. Want to come watch it?"

"Great," Tara said. "I have to pick up the dry cleaning and drop it home first. But I'll meet you at your place and I'll also spring for snacks."

"Lovely."

Not for the first time, Sameen wondered why Tara had never offered that they go to her place. Mostly they'd find something to do at the market—they'd found a tea stall that, despite being a bit ramshackle, made decent ginger tea and a variety of hot snacks, and a few times they'd hung out at Sameen's too, especially when Rohan had been out. She was starting to wonder if there was something wrong with Tara's house. Perhaps it was exceedingly messy. Or maybe she had a weird hobby she didn't want Sameen to find out about? Or perhaps it was something to do with her mother. Sameen shot a quick glance at her companion and was startled to find she was being watched.

"What's wrong?" asked Tara.

"Wrong? Nothing. Why?" Sameen replied, flustered.

"You suddenly got all serious."

Sameen smiled, a little guilty. "Some work-related thing that I remembered."

Tara nodded and looked away.

"So how long have you lived at your house?" asked Sameen, suddenly insanely curious.

"Oh, since childhood," Tara said. "It belonged to my grandparents—my mother's parents. They left it to my mother."

"Is it an old house, then?"

"About forty, fifty years, I think. I'm not sure if that's old by house standards."

"Probably not," Sameen said. "But there must be lots of memories."

"Yeah, I guess. Though it's changed a lot since my grandparents died."

"I like the older houses in the colony," Sameen put in. "Like yours. Though I've only seen it from the outside. They have more character, I feel."

"Yeah, I guess."

Tara still didn't take the hint. Sameen decided it was time to shut up.

The traffic was heavy that evening, so they got out at the end of the road. Sameen walked home and Tara went off to the dry cleaners, promising to be back in under half an hour.

Rohan and Tara had met briefly once but hadn't had an opportunity to exchange more than pleasantries. Seeing the two of them being so formal with each other was a little weird, but Sameen figured that since both were somewhat on the retiring side, it would take a few more meetings for the ice to thaw.

But at least Rohan was delighted with the samosas and onion kachoris Tara brought. "I was just thinking of making some tea," he said, trotting off to the kitchen with the brown paper bag stained with oil.

Sameen set up Rohan's twenty-one-inch iMac for them to watch *The Good Wife* on, and they soon settled around the monitor on an assortment of chairs, cradling their cups of tea.

Halfway through the episode, a screech of microphone feedback and the squawk of discordant music interrupted them. The sound equivalent to running a fingernail down a blackboard.

"What the eff!" cried Rohan. He lunged forward to pause the video.

Sameen raced to the window to see what was going on, Tara at her heels.

"Oh crap," Tara said. "Looks like a wedding."

The back of the house faced the mouth of a lane that was mostly occupied by a large temple. It wasn't particularly crowded at this time of the evening, but right now, the lane was blocked with a large green-and-red tent. They couldn't see anything through the cloth walls of the enclosure, but people were milling about. Closer to the beginning of the lane, the caterers had set up their cooking station and were chopping mounds of vegetables and firing up a tandoor for rotis.

Sameen pulled the window shut, but the wedding party's loudspeakers were potent.

"We could take the computer to the other room," Sameen suggested.

"There are no convenient plug points," Rohan pointed out.

"We could watch on my laptop," Sameen offered. "But it's a small one."

"I hate leaving something midway," Rohan said. "Let's try your laptop."

So they set up Sameen's laptop in the room farthest away from the wedding, transferred the video to it, and rigged up the speakers from the music system to boost the sound.

"Maybe it's time we got a TV," said Sameen to Rohan. "One of those fancy ones you can plug a USB stick into or connect your laptop to."

"Yeah, but what would we watch?" Rohan asked. "We do fine on the comp."

"That's true."

"You must be the first people I've ever met who don't have a TV," Tara said. "What do you do for news and stuff?"

"Duh, internet," Sameen replied. "And I can't stand the ads on TV."

"What about other stuff?" She pointed to the screen. "Like TV series?"

"We watch whatever we need online," Rohan said. "Sameen has a Netflix account and I have an Amazon Prime subscription, and there are torrents for everything else."

"Well, you certainly have your bases covered," Tara said with a laugh.

"Do you have a big-ass TV?" Sameen asked.

"Yep. A forty-inch monstrosity that my mother loves more than she loves me."

"Ooh, we should go over to yours and watch this, then."

"You'll probably have to sit through some ghastly reality show first," said Tara, rolling her eyes and helping herself to another samosa.

Sameen sighed inwardly. This was becoming quite a mystery, Tara's house.

Chapter 8

"YOU PROMISED NOT TO LAUGH!" Sameen grabbed the photo album and tucked it behind her, sticking out her lower lip in exaggeration.

"I'm sorry!" Tara tried to school her face into seriousness, but the laughter bubbled out. "I'm sorry," she said again, though she wasn't even a little bit apologetic. "It's just that I can't believe you have an album full of your childhood photos."

"Well, it's my parents'," Sameen said, letting Tara have the album back. "I brought it from Bangalore for a lark. Rohan had a blast with it."

"I can see why," Tara murmured and then immediately held up her hands. "Sorry!" She picked up her mug of coffee and took a sip. "Mm, this is good. It doesn't taste like this when I make coffee."

"Ha, don't try to win me over with flattery," Sameen said. "It's filter coffee, not the instant filth you guys are always drinking. I get it from Bangalore. Like any self-respecting south Indian, coffee is the one thing I can make."

"So who's that?" Tara pointed to a photo of a toothy teenage boy sitting on a bench with a young Sameen in a park.

"That's Milind. He's one of my closest friends. His family used to live upstairs when we were kids. I'm quite keen for you to meet him."

"He lives in Delhi?"

"Yup. Not far, he's in Green Park. But he's been flying a lot lately; he's a commercial pilot."

"You looked so different as a kid," Tara said, turning the yellowing pages of the photo album.

"Yeah, I did, didn't I? Lots of people say that to me. I wonder what changed."

Tara studied her face carefully, then looked at a photograph of a teenage Sameen. It was the same cheerful face, laughing brown eyes, frizzy hair that refused to be schooled, a wide, infectious smile. Except now those eyes that were looking back at her had a definite sensual quality. For a moment Tara was mesmerized, before she found her voice again.

"Something about your face, I think. It sort of filled out. And, of course, the braces."

Sameen grimaced. "I always hated them."

"It must be the braces—see, you look so different here."

"That's in college. Yeah, the braces were gone by then."

Tara picked up a photo of a group of young people standing by a cottage on a hillside. "Where's this?"

"Madikeri. Second-year college trip."

"Hey, Milind again, right?"

"Yep, that's him."

"It's nice that you guys have been friends for so long." Tara turned the page and stopped at another photo. "Who are these two?"

Sameen leaned forward to see. "That's Puja. She was my second-best friend at that time. And the guy is Daniel. We were," she coughed, "pretty close."

Tara's eyebrows went up. "Uh-huh?"

Sameen scrunched her eyes in thought. "As far as I recall, it all started in our first year of college, but he turned out to be such a loser eventually. In second year, a month or so after the trip, I caught him holding hands with Puja by the storage area behind the canteen."

"Ouch," said Tara. "Holding hands and all?"

"Yeah." Sameen made a face. "I know. But still. I broke up with both of them."

"Did you have any other boyfriends?" asked Tara. "Before Rohan, I mean."

"Oh yeah. When I was doing my master's degree, there was this guy, Farhan—the son of some family friends. He was nice, but a bit boring. After a couple of months, we realized our families were trying to set us up and we decided to part ways amicably. My mother was heartbroken."

Tara smiled. "Sounds familiar."

"And after that, a few years before I met Rohan, there was this fellow." Sameen leafed through the album in front of her. "I don't think I have a photo of him. I was so smitten with him, but now I can't even remember his name—Anish, Avinash... something like that."

"What happened?"

Sameen sighed. "He came to the office one day with a stack of invitation cards—to his wedding."

That made Tara laugh. "Poor you."

"Of course, all this is not counting the heartbreaks suffered over cricketers and movie stars."

"Of course."

Under normal circumstances, Tara would never have steered the conversation here, but her curiosity about Sameen's past had ushered her down this dangerous path. And yet, when it led to the inevitable question, it still caught her off guard.

"And what about you?" Sameen asked. "Tell me about your deep, dark past. You have no life, so I'm assuming you're currently unattached."

"Hey, I have a life." She tried to look outraged. But her heart was suddenly thumping out of her chest.

"Don't derail the subject," Sameen said firmly. "Do you have a secret beau stuffed away somewhere?"

Tara shook her head, smiling. "Secret *beau*? No, no, nothing like that." She sat up and tucked her legs underneath her. *This is it, I have to tell her now.* She stared at her hands. "It's not quite like that."

"Then what is it like? Oh my god, you're already married in secret?"

Tara burst out laughing. "No, of course not."

"Then?"

She looked up at Sameen, who rocked forward, all ears. Tara felt calm all of a sudden. She thought of the time she had gone white-water rafting with her friends, the sudden stillness after the rush of the rapids.

This wasn't something she necessarily shared about herself. She didn't think it was anyone else's business. But she did have an instinct that told her when it was safe to talk about, and right now she felt safe.

"There isn't much to tell. Only that I'm gay."

Tara could be inscrutable at the best of times, but this was something different. Sameen could tell she was waiting for a response. And the wrong one, or one that took too long to come, would be a disaster.

"I'm sorry," Sameen heard herself say. "I thought I heard you say you're gay."

"That's exactly what I said," Tara replied, her voice calm, but her fingers tapped the album.

Sameen stared at her, wide-eyed. "No. Really?"

Ugh. Why were her brain and her mouth not connected?

"Yep. Really."

"Oh wow." It still felt ridiculous and inadequate as a response, but Sameen felt like all the air had gone out of her at Tara's confession. "I...I'd never have guessed. Since when?"

Tara looked at her like she'd lost her mind. "Um...since always."

"No, no," Sameen hastened to elaborate. "I meant...I don't know what I meant. You just took me by surprise."

She rested her head against the wall, studying Tara. The photo album lay forgotten on her lap. "You know, knowing Milind all these years has honed my gaydar to almost one hundred per cent accuracy. I can't believe it missed picking you up."

Tara gave a crooked smile and shook her head. "We-ell, I've had many years of practice hiding it."

Sameen nodded in understanding. "Let me rephrase my earlier question, then," she said with a glint in her eyes. "Do you have a secret girlfriend tucked away somewhere?"

Tara crossed her arms. "Not for many years."

"How come?"

"I just wasn't interested, I guess."

"What do you mean?" Sameen was getting increasingly more puzzled by Tara's replies.

"It means I don't ever want to be in a relationship."

Okay, that was the most curious thing Sameen had ever heard. "What? Why?"

"In this country? It's pointless."

Pointless. That took Sameen aback. She'd never heard it described that way, not even when she'd stood by Milind during all the ups and downs in his life. She'd seen him come to terms with his sexuality, fall in love, and get his heart broken. She'd been devastated for him because of the hostility he'd faced from his family, and terrified because the law was not on his side. But he'd never said anything about it being pointless. Ever.

Not even when his family had more or less disowned him after he'd told them they should stop dropping hints about suitable women for him to marry. He'd never actually come out to them in a straightforward manner, but he had implied it. Neither had they officially cut him off. They'd just implied back that it would be better for them all if he kept his distance.

Yet Milind hadn't given up living his life on his terms. He'd been with Ashish for five years now. They seemed so perfect for each other—though there was a tiny possibility Sameen was biased—and they seemed contented. All their friends knew about them. Even Sameen's parents seemed to have some inkling, given the veiled questions her mother often asked about whether Milind was "happy".

She didn't want to make Tara uncomfortable, so she kept her mouth shut. But there *was* something else she was curious to know.

"Why did you tell me about this? Not that I'm complaining."

"Apart from Barkha, you're my only friend and I wanted you to know. I guess I would've told you eventually, because even though I ignore it and have no need for it, it is still a part of me."

"Of course you would've told me. You're an open book, waiting to pour your heart out at the slightest opportunity."

Tara smacked Sameen's arm with the photo album. "And you are very rude."

Sameen scrunched her nose. "This is so funny."

"What?"

"That both my best friends are gay."

Tara's eyes narrowed in mock disapproval. "Are you now going to ask me if we know each other?"

Sameen poked her with her toe. "You don't?" she said, batting her eyes in mock wonder. "How *come*?"

Tara shook her head. She didn't seem upset, so Sameen relaxed. "Can I ask you another question?"

Tara shrugged. "I think we're long past that stage where you need permission."

"What happens if you fall in love?"

"It's not going to happen. I won't let it." Tara's determination was baffling.

"You can't control it, you know. It just happens."

"I can," she said with vehemence.

Well, what can you say to that?

She sighed. "Oh Tara, you have no romantic bone in your body."

"And you're full of fluff. I've seen all the Mills and Boons you own." She turned around to look at Sameen's bookshelf.

"Hey, if you had to read and edit books by people like Loveleen Bing day in and day out, you would start reading fluff too."

"I doubt it. Definitely not fluff about straight people. Yuck!"

"Fine. Whatever." Sameen stuck her tongue out at Tara and got up from the sofa. "I'm going to get more coffee. Want?"

"Sure."

At the door, Sameen turned around. Tara's attention was back on the album. For a moment or two, Sameen watched her, an unexpected warmth filling her. Tara had said Sameen was her only other friend.

Chapter 9

"LET'S CATCH THAT MOVIE TONIGHT," Milind said.

"You just got back last week. Don't you want to spend time with Ashish?" Sameen asked.

"Our boyfriends can live without us for one evening."

"Rohan left this morning for that Japan thing. You don't remember anything I tell you. Anyway, I can't. I promised Tara I'd show her that momo shop that also makes these spiral potato chips."

"You and your new BFF," he said with a sniff. "I go away for a bit and you've already replaced me."

"Stop it, drama queen. We can go for the movie tomorrow, all three of us. You and Tara can meet each other too." She felt a little guilty because she and Tara had already discussed watching the movie Milind wanted to see. He was right—she had been ignoring him lately. And he had every right to be upset. He was, after all, a very dear friend.

"So, getting free taxi rides these days, huh?" Milind went on. "This Tara is one forgiving girl, I must say, giving lifts to her hijacker."

Of course, he could also be very tiresome sometimes.

"That joke is getting quite old now. And it's not free. We share."

She got off the phone and started getting her things together to leave. Her phone rang once, then stopped. It was a missed call from Tara—their signal that she should come to the gate. Sameen picked up her bag and ran down the stairs. She was hungry—momos would be perfect today.

Usually, as soon as Rohan left town, she'd start making plans to meet up with all her friends, especially Milind, so she wouldn't miss Rohan too much. But this morning after he'd left, Sameen hadn't felt the familiar restlessness. She hadn't called anyone or made plans to catch up with them. She wondered why that was.

Deep in thought, she jogged down the steps. It was only a fraction of a second after she was falling that she realized the heel of her shoe—a modest inch-high one at that—had twisted under her. Sameen made a grab for the hand rail, but missed. She fell awkwardly, slipping down the last few steps and tumbling to the landing.

Winded and bewildered, Sameen lay there. A few seconds could have passed or a few minutes before she gathered her wits and remembered Tara was waiting. With the help of the railing, she pulled herself up. Excruciating pain ripped through her right ankle, and she cried out as she collapsed again, dizzy from the pain.

Most people in the building had left for the day and the stairwell was empty. Her purse had fallen open, and her pens and phone had slipped out. Music was playing somewhere. Sameen realized it was her phone. She reached for it, seeing Tara's name on the display. "Tara, I fell," she managed to gasp. "It really hurts."

Tara didn't offer any platitudes. "Where are you?"

"Stairs."

"Stay there. Don't move."

Even if she'd wanted to, Sameen couldn't. It hurt too much. Not just her ankle, but also her back. She sat on the landing, propping her elbow on the stairs so she could lean at an angle that was most comfortable. She remembered reading somewhere about patterned breathing, which helped with pain. She closed her eyes and tried to take regular shallow breaths. Then she remembered where she'd read it—a magazine article on how to deal with labour pains.

I don't care, she told herself. *Pain is pain.*

The patterned breathing did help; at least it helped her zone out. She had only a vague recollection of what happened next. She remembered Tara appearing with a security guard. She remembered being helped into the taxi. She remembered putting her head on Tara's shoulder and feeling safe. Then she shut her eyes.

Tara sank down in the only available seat in the waiting area of the hospital's emergency department and leaned back against the wall. She closed her eyes, forcing herself to relax and give in to the sense of relief she could finally let herself feel.

As soon as she'd heard Sameen's voice on the phone, she'd switched to autopilot and had done everything she could to make sure Sameen received help as soon as possible. In the taxi, she'd realized Sameen was in no real danger, though watching her grimace through her pain had been distressing. Tara had hated the fact that she hadn't been able to do anything to make Sameen feel better. The situation had brought out a fierce protective instinct in her that she hadn't ever thought she possessed.

But this wasn't the time to dwell on all that. She had other matters to take care of.

Though Sameen's condition wasn't serious, Tara needed to let people close to Sameen know. She knew that Rohan had left for some training course abroad, so she called the only other person she knew of in Sameen's life—her friend Milind. Sameen had said he was a pilot, so Tara hoped he wasn't away flying a plane to some far-off destination.

As it turned out, he wasn't, and he arrived at the hospital, panting, in exactly twenty minutes.

"What happened?" Milind asked, his eyes wide with worry.

"She slipped on the stairs. She's in a lot of pain, so I suspect she might have broken something."

"Have the docs seen her?"

Tara shook her head. "Still in line."

Milind went to speak to Sameen in her little green-curtained cubicle, but came out almost immediately. "Seems to be asleep."

"Yeah, she's pretty dazed."

He plopped down into a seat next to Tara. "Thanks for taking care of her and bringing her here." Then he looked a bit abashed. "I don't mean to imply you would have abandoned her, of course."

Tara shook her head. "Don't worry about it. I just hope it's nothing serious."

"Yeah."

They sat together in tense silence, Tara impatient that they were taking so long to see Sameen. She glanced at Milind. He had a dishevelled air about him, but that could just be because he'd rushed there. His hair looked like he'd run his fingers through it many times, and he had a scar on the bridge of his nose. He was tall, tall enough that he had to fold himself awkwardly in the hospital seat, and thin. He had a rip in the left knee of his jeans that didn't look as though it had been put there by design. She knew he and Sameen were close, but didn't know much else about him.

"I wish we didn't have to meet in these circumstances," he said, startling her. It was like he'd read her mind. But then, Tara figured, if she'd been studying him, he had all the more reason to be sizing her up.

"What? Yeah, I know."

A harried nurse rushed towards the cubicle that Sameen was in. "Sameen Siddiqi?" she called, looking at the waiting area.

"Yes," Tara and Milind said in tandem, jumping up.

Two doctors arrived almost immediately to examine Sameen, and things moved quickly from then on. X-rays confirmed Sameen's ankle had a hairline fracture and she had also bruised her back. Her right leg, from just below her knee, was put in a cast, which she would have to keep on for four weeks. She was also advised rest.

It was past nine by the time they were discharged. Milind had a car and drove them home. Sameen was groggy, the effect of painkillers this time, and it took a lot of manoeuvring by Tara and Milind to get her up the stairs.

"Will you help her get into bed while I go and see if there's anything to eat?" Milind asked Tara, wiping sweat from his brow.

"Sure."

Tara helped Sameen sit at the edge of the bed. With tentative hands she pulled Sameen's blouse off, making sure her hands didn't come in contact with Sameen's body. Eyes averted, she got the T-shirt she'd found hanging behind the door, and helped Sameen get into it. She then looked in the direction of her next task—Sameen's skirt—wishing Milind was handling the undressing part while she was the one taking care of the food. She somehow managed to get Sameen's skirt off and help her into track pants, and finally into bed. Then she breathed a huge sigh of relief.

Milind appeared with a tray that contained a mug of soup and a couple of slices of buttered toast. Sameen moaned about not being hungry, but they managed to coax her into eating one slice and most of the soup. There were more medicines to be given, and when Sameen finally dropped into a deep, undisturbed sleep, Milind and Tara looked at each other with relief and collapsed on the sofa in the living room.

Tara rubbed her eyes. "Maybe we should order some food," she said, looking at the time. It was almost eleven.

"Good idea." Milind produced a stash of home-delivery menus, and after some calling around, they found a place that delivered pizzas till midnight.

As they waited for the food, Tara knew they'd have to talk about the situation. Sameen clearly couldn't be left by herself. At least not tonight.

"I was thinking," Milind said, "someone should stay with her tonight."

He can't actually read minds, can he? Tara wondered. "I was thinking the same."

"I have a morning flight out tomorrow. I can call and tell them there was an emergency…"

"No, don't do that," said Tara. "I'll stay with her."

"I can't ask you to do that."

"You're not. I live almost next door, so it's not a problem."

"But you have to go to work too."

"Not till late tomorrow. Do you know anyone else who could come and stay while I'm in office? I can come back in the evening."

"I can get Ashish to take over tomorrow morning. And I'll also get him to rally our other friends around."

"That'd be great. Don't worry about food and all—I'll arrange that. And I'm very close by, so I can look in every evening, maybe even stay if needed."

Chapter 10

WHEN SAMEEN WOKE THE NEXT morning, her ankle was throbbing again and she felt a painful stiffness in her back. Someone was huddled on the bed next to her, curled up at the very edge. She thought it would be Milind, but when the person shifted and turned, she saw it was Tara.

"Hey," Tara said gently.

"Where's Milind?"

"He had to get home—he had an early flight. How are you feeling?"

"Like I fell down the stairs." Sameen pulled herself upright gingerly. Her back twinged in protest. "Tara, I'm so sorry for causing all this trouble."

Tara sat up too. She was wearing a faded T-shirt and three-quarter pyjamas. She had probably gone home to get some of her stuff.

"Don't be silly," she said.

"No, really. And I'm really grateful you're here. And that you stay so near. Because I don't know what I'd do, with Rohan away and all."

"Listen, Milind and I have been working out a system to make sure someone stays with you," Tara said. "So stop stressing. And, as you say, I live virtually next door." She stood and stretched. "Now, what would madam like for breakfast?"

Even though she still had some pain and a lot of discomfort, Sameen found, to her relief, that she could move around by herself. By the time she'd freshened up and Tara had made tea and omelettes for breakfast, Ashish arrived, armed with a stainless-steel multi-tiered tiffin box.

"I've got lunch," he said, setting it on the table. "And I can stay till the evening."

"I've just broken my foot. I'm not dying," Sameen protested.

"Great," Tara said. "I can be back by seven. Would that be okay for you?"

"Absolutely," Ashish replied.

"Hey, hello?" Sameen waved both hands, slightly irritated. "I said, I'm not dying."

"And we'd like to keep it that way," Ashish said.

Despite Sameen's protests, over the next few weeks, her friends adjusted their lives around her. Fortunately, she was relatively mobile and didn't need help around the house, and thankfully everyone realized she didn't require twenty-four-hour minding. So she was usually by herself during the day, but every evening one of her other friends came over, and either Milind or Tara always stayed the night.

They'd also managed to work some sort of arrangement to make sure Sameen had food so she wouldn't have to cook. "Rather, so you don't live on instant noodles," as Milind had put it. On most days, he cooked dinner or Tara brought some over. When he was away on flight duty, Tara was usually around, even if other people dropped by. They also made sure Sameen had breakfast, lunch, and snacks for the next day so she could get as much rest as possible.

A cleaner came around daily, so that was taken care of. Sameen had talked to her boss the day after the accident, who had agreed to let her work part-time from home till she could return to the office. And, of course, her friends plied her with entertainment—books and DVDs. When Sameen crossed her monthly internet limit streaming TV series, Tara gave her her data card. She still hadn't got her head around the fact Rohan and Sameen didn't have a TV. "Who doesn't have a TV?" she complained to Sameen, who laughed.

"The good thing about you going away," Sameen told Rohan on Skype one day, "is that I've realized what a fantastic bunch of friends I have, especially Tara. She's been so wonderful, Ro. I feel like I've known her forever."

"So you're not missing me?"

"Not at all." Sameen stuck her tongue out at him. She felt sorry for him because he looked so forlorn and helpless. "I have Tara now." And it was true. She wasn't just saying it to tease Rohan; imagining her life without Tara these last few weeks was quite impossible.

Rohan shook his head. "Well, don't get too attached. I will be back in a week. Got to go now. Say hi to Tara. Love you."

Sameen sent him a beating-heart emoji in response via the text message box and logged off. She got to her feet using her crutches and went in search of Tara.

It was really sweet how Tara always made herself scarce whenever she and Rohan Skyped.

The weeks passed and Tara was oddly content with their weird little routine. She got no pleasure out of cooking and doing housework generally, but lending a hand around Sameen's place felt different. Thanks to Rohan's housekeeping skills, the house was impeccably organized, which helped. And Sameen's company was invigorating. They watched tonnes and tonnes of TV shows and movies, some good, some extremely questionable, and got into friendly tussles about which stories were interesting and which were rubbish. They talked and talked—about all sorts of things, from the Syrian refugee crisis, Hindu fundamentalism, and Donald Trump, to cricket and PV Sindhu.

Despite the turn of events that had left Sameen housebound, Tara had to admit she was as happy as could be. Sometimes she felt a stab of guilt thinking that she was using Sameen's misfortune as an excuse to add excitement to her mundane routine of home, office, home, office, rinse and repeat. But she couldn't deny that she had never before so looked forward to coming back home in the evenings, and never had such a rapt audience as Sameen as she vented about office politics and the idiocy of her junior colleagues. And never before had evenings spent in front of the TV—well, technically a computer monitor—been so engaging.

The only awkward moments were when Rohan Skyped. Even though Tara made sure to vanish when that happened, there were times—if she were being completely honest—she resented those twenty minutes or so that she could hear their incoherent mumblings from the other room. She knew she was being unreasonable, but Rohan felt like an intruder in their blissful existence.

One day, Tara had a brainwave. She came over with a large cardboard box.

Sameen raised her eyebrows quizzically. "What's that?"

"A jigsaw puzzle," said Tara. "I'm sick of watching stuff. It's so passive. Let's put our brains to work."

"It's not passive—we analyse the stuff we watch."

"In other words, you rip apart every tiny little plot hole."

"And you are too forgiving."

"Fine then, no more watching. It's jigsaw time."

Tara placed a stool for Sameen to rest her leg on and cleared the dining table, on which she spread out the jigsaw pieces. It was the massive 1,000-piece *Casablanca* puzzle she'd never got around to restarting and would clearly take them days to finish.

"We should watch the movie," Sameen said.

"You can watch it when Milind is here," Tara said firmly.

Two hours later, Tara revised her opinion. "I think it's going to take us *years* to finish this."

"Good. That means you have to keep coming around for years."

"Why would I not come around?" Tara asked in surprise.

Sameen pursed her lips. "But, you know, now you'll *have* to." She gave Tara a crooked smile. "And to seal the deal, I suggest we get pizza."

"Done." Tara hoisted herself out of the chair to get her phone, which was charging in the other room. "I'm just glad you're not sick of me," she said at the door to the living room, as casually as she could manage. Because the idea Sameen wanted to make sure Tara would keep coming over for years gave her a warm and fuzzy feeling.

"Sick of you?" Sameen said, her eyes half-closed. "Never. Not until we've watched all the TV shows in the world."

Tara smiled.

The pizza came and they set up a British comedy called *Miranda* to watch with dinner—conveniently forgetting they'd decided to give up TV. But it was hilarious and they laughed so much that their sides ached. The pizza was gone in no time at all and they were still hungry, so Tara ran across to the bakery down the road for muffins.

It was a chilly night, so they spread a light Jaipuri quilt over their legs, eating their muffins with paper napkins tucked under their chins. When the last episode of *Miranda* had streamed, they were leaning against each other, exhausted from laughing. Tara looked down at Sameen, whose eyes were almost closed, resting on her shoulder.

"This was a very nice evening," Sameen said.

"It was," Tara said, smiling down at her.

Something had been different about today. Something Tara couldn't quite define, a contentment she couldn't ever recall having felt before. She reached out and brushed a strand of hair off Sameen's forehead, her fingers trailing down her cheek for just a moment.

A fraction of a second later, she realized what she'd done.

Tara froze. In fact, everything froze, inside her and out. The next half a second was like an eternity, when time almost slowed to a standstill, the earth stopped moving, and everything, absolutely everything, made sense with devastating clarity.

She wanted much more than to just brush a strand of hair from Sameen's face. She couldn't run from it any more—her feelings for Sameen had long since strayed over the line of control that she had been calling friendship. Tara had thought that as long as she called Sameen that—a friend—she would be in control, but she hadn't banked on meeting someone who would slowly take down her walls brick by brick without her being aware of it.

The feelings she had been certain she had a tight grip on had only turned out to be fine sand, gradually seeping between her fingers till she was left clutching at air.

A wave of panic welled up inside her.

Sameen remained still, a tranquil smile on her face, her eyes closed. Tara resisted the impulse to jump away. Instead, with deliberate, slow movements, she pushed Sameen upright. "I... er...should clear up."

Tara grabbed the napkins and the empty pizza boxes and rushed to the kitchen. She pressed the bottoms of her palms into her eyes.

"Shit! Shit! Shit!"

"Tara?" Sameen called. "Can you lend a hand with the sheets?"

"Coming."

Tara helped Sameen make the bed in silence. She couldn't even meet her eyes.

"Something wrong?" Sameen asked. "You've gone very quiet."

"No, no. Just remembered something about work."

After getting Sameen settled in bed, Tara went into the bathroom and sat on the lid of the toilet, head in her hands.

She took a deep breath. "Calm down, Tara," she said. "Relax."

There was no need to panic, she told herself as she took a few deep breaths. Nothing had really happened. She had just brushed a strand of hair from Sameen's face. Hardly inappropriate. No reason to beat herself up or imagine Sameen would ostracize her for it. Sameen was one of her best friends. They had had a good time together, they were comfortable with each other... The panic bubbled again.

She needed to get out of here. She needed some space, and anyway, the thought of spending the night next to Sameen on her bed, the thought of her rolling over so their arms and legs touched…it was unbearable.

A sob escaped her. Her hands shaking, she dialled Milind's number.

"Hey, sorry to drop this on you so suddenly, but I, er, have a work thing…emergency." Tara hadn't expected her voice to be so steady, so calm, so in control. "Could you take over at Sameen's place? … Yeah, right away … You can? … Oh, thanks, Milind, thanks so much."

Tara washed her face and left the bathroom. Sameen was fast asleep when Tara checked on her. The half an hour or so Milind took to arrive felt like the longest in Tara's life. Part of her was relieved she didn't have to say good-bye to Sameen, even though a twinge of guilt curled around her. She felt guilty about lying to Milind too, but she didn't know what else to do. Thank god Rohan would be back in a couple of days and this rigmarole of spending half her life at Sameen's would stop.

When she got into bed at home, sleep was a long time coming.

Chapter 11

"YOU HAVE TO STOP SPENDING so much time with him." Tara struggled to keep her voice down. The smell of re-fried samosas in the college canteen was making her sick.

Radhika pecked at the sandwich they were supposedly sharing. "We are working on a project together. How do you expect me to do that if I don't talk to him?"

"I take the same class. I'm working on the same project with a partner. I don't spend all my free evenings with him. Don't pretend this is all about work."

"I'm not pretending. It's the truth."

Tara's hands balled into fists. "Don't lie to me!"

"Calm down. You're creating a scene."

"You're one to talk."

"Tara, you're being completely unreasonable."

Tara banged her fist on the table. "You started this."

Radhika winced, taking a quick, surreptitious look around. "What's wrong with you?"

"Fine then, if you don't want to talk about it..." She stood.

Radhika caught her hand. "Please, Tara, just listen to me. Please."

Tara glowered but she sat down reluctantly.

Radhika placed her palms on the table and leaned forward. "I am not interested in Amandeep," she said in a low voice. "I love you. I want only you. He is just my friend and classmate. That's it."

A tear rolled down Tara's cheek. She brushed it angrily aside. "You are going to leave me for him. I just know it."

"How can you say that? We've been together for more than a year. Hasn't it meant anything to you?"

"Of course it has. But I doubt it meant anything to you. I've been just fun and games for you. Now that you have a man in your life, you can seriously start thinking about building your future with him."

"You're being completely ridiculous now. You are my future. Not him."

"What future are you talking about? In this society? In this country? You think we can live together or get married?"

"Not get married maybe, but yes, we can live together. A lot of other people like us do."

"I don't care about other people. What are you going to tell your parents? What am I going to tell my parents?"

"Hang on. Wasn't this about me being friends with Amandeep? How has this suddenly become about society?"

"These are very real questions. We don't live in a bubble."

"We don't have to worry about all this right now. I'm sure we can find a way to deal with it when the time comes."

"I'm not so sure. I don't think I can do this any more."

"Yes, you can. Give it some time. Just let's get through this project. Everything will go back to normal. You'll see."

Tara shook her head. "Nothing will ever be the same." She got up again and walked towards the door. The tears kept coming. This time she did not stop when Radhika called her name.

That was a decade ago, but Tara still remembered it like yesterday. At that time, walking away from Radhika had been the hardest thing she had done in her twenty-year-old life, but time had mended her broken heart. Radhika had pursued Tara relentlessly for months after that conversation in the canteen, but Tara hadn't given in. She had been convinced they could never have had a future together. And she still thought she had made the right decision.

Tara was in her early adolescence when she got a sense that she was different. She had not shared her friends' growing interest in boys, but she had spent a lot of time mooning over a particular senior who travelled with her in the school bus, even though she never talked to Tara. It all came together one day when she had been watching an American TV series where they mentioned the word "lesbian". Something about it had rung a bell and the thirteen-year-old Tara had pulled out a dictionary to look it up. One meaning had led to her looking up other words, and many things made sense to her that day. Though she had been relieved that a term existed to describe the way she felt, her feelings weren't something she'd spent too much time thinking about. She'd had too many other interests that occupied her.

That is, until she had met Radhika when she was eighteen and had just entered college. Suddenly, her whole world had shifted. Feelings she hadn't known existed overwhelmed her and took her to places she'd never been. In a matter of months, they had gone from classmates to friends to lovers. Tara had discovered love.

But whereas the young Tara had accepted her sexuality with equanimity, the newly adult Tara had freaked out. She couldn't help comparing her relationship to the freedom her straight friends took for granted—the way they could flaunt their partners, for instance. Even though she'd realized that if she looked carefully, she'd be sure to find other gay people around her, she was aware how different things would be for them.

Tara had subsequently made a secret project of ferreting out all the literature she could on homosexuality and how gay people lived around the world. She'd read about civil rights struggles not just in India, but elsewhere as well. Later on, when Section 377 was read down, she celebrated by buying herself a silver bracelet. And when the Supreme Court had reinstated the colonial law, reversing the earlier decision and re-criminalizing gay sex, she had cried into her pillow.

Back in university, she'd had her antenna out about how those around her talked about gay people. The more she'd learnt, the angrier and more afraid she'd become. She had hated keeping her relationship with Radhika a secret, yet she had seen no way they could ever tell anyone about it. In fact, what was the point? They couldn't exactly walk into the sunset together, hand in hand. Actually, Tara wasn't sure what she was looking for. True, her parents weren't ultra-conservative, but she just couldn't be sure how they would react.

Sex and sexuality were not topics that were discussed in their house. Talking about homosexuality wasn't exactly taboo. In fact, to say it was in a pre-taboo stage—way beyond her parents' imagination—would be more accurate. They might've read about it in newspapers and books, and heard it referred to on television shows, but it was always far removed from their lives, and Tara didn't know where to begin having this conversation with them. She wasn't exactly dying to pour her heart out to her family, but it would have been nice if what she felt for Radhika didn't seem so awkward and unwieldy.

Breaking up with Radhika had then become an inevitability. In her heart of hearts, she had known it wasn't Amandeep that was the problem—it was society, and she had no stomach to fight it. The pain and guilt of the break-up were enormous, and it had left her devastated, but she had been convinced she had done the right thing and saved herself from inevitable heartache later. Because, clearly, there was no future for her as one half of a lesbian couple.

Of course, there was always the option of migrating somewhere with a more liberal outlook towards homosexuality, but this was her home and she had no intention of leaving it. That left the only other option: to marry someone of the opposite sex and live a socially approved life.

Tara did, however, understand that marrying a man she didn't love would not only destroy her life, but also his. So she had managed to pack up her guilt, confusion, and anger, put them into a box, and seal them deep inside her. She promised herself to stay away from anything that could lead to her developing romantic or sexual feelings for anyone. And she had been quite successful in sticking to that resolve.

Then Sameen had come along. What was it about her that had unwrapped Tara's carefully boxed-up life without her being aware of it?

I can't believe this is happening to me, Tara thought, as yet another sleepless night stretched on in which the same thoughts roiled around in her head.

That night at Sameen's and that brief intimate touch had shaken her. So far, Tara had managed to distance herself whenever she'd noticed an attraction to another woman. But what had gone wrong with Sameen and why had it felt so right? Tara didn't have an answer. She only knew she could no longer deny that she had feelings for Sameen.

The more Tara tried to push the images of Sameen out of her head, the more they flooded her. That moonlit walk home when they'd both been a bit tipsy. How stunning Sameen had looked in her sari, with her gold earrings and her hair done up. The way they stayed up late so many nights at Sameen's place, talking about anything. That little bubble of happiness she felt when Sameen would hurry through the gate and hop into the cab. The way she looked forward to their evening plans. That first sight of Sameen standing under the bus stop, and her smile. The way her heart would give a little flop when her phone beeped and it was Sameen with a message or call.

Oh my god! How could I have let this happen?

But worrying about these questions was pointless. It wasn't like the answers were going to matter because Tara had no plans to explore them in any greater depth. And if she had been tempted to, she just had to remind herself that Sameen was straight and in a committed relationship. She was straight. Straight!

Tara knew what she had to do. She had to nip it in the bud. And the only way to do that was to stay away from Sameen Siddiqi.

When Sameen had woken to find Milind rather than Tara in the house, with some story about Tara having a work emergency, she hadn't thought too much of it, apart from feeling a smidge of disappointment that Tara had gone without a good-bye.

"We had such fun last night," she'd told Milind, looking at the mess of the jigsaw on the dining table. "First there was the jigsaw, then we got pizza and watched this *hilarious* comedy."

Tara hadn't turned up that evening. She hadn't even called—just sent a message to ask if Sameen was okay. The next day, Rohan had come back and there was so much to talk about and settle him back that the days went by. Sameen was puzzled at Tara's continued absence, but with her lack of mobility and Rohan fussing over her, she couldn't exactly chase Tara down. But that didn't mean that Sameen wasn't a little bit hurt.

Of course, Tara had really stepped up when Sameen had needed her, and Sameen was inordinately grateful. Those few weeks had also clearly separated her real friends from the fair-weather ones. Normally surrounded by people, she had been quite taken aback when they had slowly become very busy in her time of need, leaving only Milind, Ashish, and Tara.

Now, a fortnight later, when she was finally and officially mobile, smoking out Tara was Sameen's number-one priority.

They'd barely exchanged a word in this time, nothing apart from a few hurried texts. Tara's work schedule seemed to have exploded, seemingly leaving her with no room for a social life. Heck, no room for a life. A website relaunch and preparing for the Davis Cup coverage, whatever sport that was, was all very well, but how could she disappear just like that? Especially after they'd become so close. And, more than anything, she had filled a hole in Sameen's life that she hadn't even known existed.

When Sameen had moved to Delhi three years ago to pursue her ambition of being in the frontline of publishing, she'd had to leave her home and the friends she had grown up with back in Bangalore. Always used to being surrounded with people, she had been miserable until Milind had also moved to Delhi. They'd shared a flat for a year or so, till he decided to move in with Ashish. Sameen had lived on her own for another year before she and Rohan decided to live together. Of course, she had made other friends in the meantime, but Tara had been different from all of them. In just a few months, Sameen had felt a closeness with her that she hadn't with anyone else in her adult life.

And then the damn woman had vanished. Which had left Sameen with only one option—to hunt her down.

She put her hands on the low iron gate and studied the car that took up most of the space in the small courtyard. The red-brick building had three floors and a terrace. A nameplate next to the gate said, "Dixits, Ground Floor." Sameen wondered who lived on the other two floors.

She stretched her ankle. This was the longest walk she'd taken since her accident. Her foot seemed fine, though. She glanced at her watch—Tara should be home by now. She unlatched the gate, went up to the door, and rang the bell. A few seconds later, an older woman opened the door and looked quizzically at her.

"Is Tara at home?" Sameen asked politely.

"No, she's not back yet. Is she expecting you?"

The woman was clearly Tara's mother. They had the same eyes and the same way of slightly tilting the head when asking a question.

"I'm Sameen, her friend, I live—"

"Oh, you're Sameen?" Tara's mother broke into a happy smile. "How's your foot, dear? Come in, don't stand there. Did you walk all the way here? Oh my! Are you all right? Sit down. Shall I make you some tea? Water?"

Sameen blinked. She suddenly had second thoughts about this garrulous woman being related to the reticent Tara. "I, er, I'm fine, Aunty."

"Aunty? Psh. My name is Chhaya—you can call me that. We're all adults here."

Sameen was ushered into a neat living room. The first thing she noticed was the giant TV. She hadn't realized how big forty inches was. It sort of made sense now why Tara had been appalled she didn't have a TV. The second thing she noticed was a half-finished jigsaw puzzle on the dining table.

Chhaya went to fetch her a glass of water. "Tara should be home in a bit. Will you have some tea?"

"Oh no, Aunt... Chhaya, don't trouble yourself. I just wanted to check in on Tara. I haven't seen her for a couple of weeks, so just wanted to say hi and catch up."

"You haven't seen her for two weeks? Why?"

"She's been so busy, you know. The relaunch and all."

Chhaya frowned, looking bemused. "Relaunch?" Then she shook her head. "Uff, this girl. I never know what goes on in her head. Never mind her. You're here now and Tara talks so much about you. Let's have some tea—I was going to make some anyway."

The tea was made—Sameen helped—and a plate of cumin biscuits appeared. Chhaya was quite the chatterbox and admitted that Tara had inherited her retiring personality from her father, who had died of a heart attack a few years ago. She looked sad when she spoke of how close he and Tara had been, and how his passing had seemed to put a light out in Tara.

"But I was so happy when she made friends with you," she said. "It's like she started to have a life again instead of sitting around watching TV and doing jigsaws all day."

Sameen glanced around the living room. Now that she was finally getting to see the inside of Tara's home, Sameen wondered why she had been so cagey about it. The heavy wooden furniture reminded Sameen of her own parents' home. The space had a comfortable, lived-in feel to it, not like the sterile, shining homes some people preferred, with not a pin out of place.

She also admired the building itself and said so to Chhaya. It was old but wonderfully maintained. She wondered again why Tara had never invited her here. If Sameen had a house like this, she'd have people over all the time.

Tara's mother kept up a non-stop chatter till there was the sound of a key turning at the door.

"Tara, come and see who's here," Chhaya called out.

Tara's face peered around the door.

"Hellooo!" Sameen grinned at her.

Tara seemed to freeze. She stared at Sameen, nonplussed, inhaling loudly. Her eyes roved the entire room, taking in the living room and dining area. Whatever she saw, or didn't see, clearly passed muster, because she relaxed visibly. But not completely.

Sameen stared at Tara, an uneasy feeling bubbling inside her. Why was Tara not happy to see her? What was going on?

"Hey, Sameen," she said, plastering on a smile that was a bit too bright to be natural. "You're up and about?"

"Yes, just got cleared to go out today," Sameen said, searching Tara's serious, dark eyes for an answer. Any answer. "How are you?"

"I'm fine."

Tara didn't even meet Sameen's gaze. She appeared tired and drawn. Sameen was used to seeing her after a long day at work but didn't remember her ever being this worn out. The way she stood uncertainly at the doorway of her own house was also odd.

"Sameen has just agreed to stay for dinner," Chhaya told her daughter. "I've made chicken, and we can quickly make some chapatis."

"Oh, er...great," Tara said.

Chhaya stood. "Now that you're back, I'm going to go to the tailor and see if the curtains are done." She nudged Tara as she passed her and said in a sibilant whisper, "Such a lovely girl. Why haven't you brought her around before?"

Chapter 12

Tara got herself a glass of water and went to sit on the chair at right angles to the sofa Sameen was perched on. She took a few deep breaths, raised her glance from the mug in Sameen's hand to her face, and braved a little smile.

"So. Back to the land of the living?" Tara asked.

Her heart hammered fit to burst out of her ribcage. Sameen was a sight for sore eyes. How Tara had missed her. Friends weren't exactly crawling out of the woodwork for her, but the few she had meant a lot. But there had never been a Complication—capital C—like this one before.

"I am, but you've gone into some dark and distant place yourself." Sameen leaned forward and caught Tara's arm. "Are you all right?"

Tara's head and heart rebelled, tearing at each other. Her resolve to keep her distance, built up and hardened over the past fortnight, started to buckle.

"Ye...yes, I'm all right, just..."

"Busy, I know, you keep saying, but Tara, you look terrible. You'll fall sick at this rate."

Tara gripped the glass of water in her lap. If only Sameen knew how messed up she'd been feeling. But given the way she was leaning towards her, her face contorted in a worried frown, Tara couldn't help feeling that maybe she had been making a big deal out of nothing.

Tara wanted to catch her by the shoulders and drink her in. Fill that void that the past fortnight had been.

Stop it!

Sameen let go of Tara's arm and sank back into the sofa. "Can I ask you something?"

"Sure."

"It's been worrying me for a while," Sameen said slowly, "the way...you left so suddenly. I...it wasn't me, was it? Did I say something stupid when I was high on painkillers or something?"

Tara let out a guffaw. She couldn't help herself—a consequence perhaps of the pent-up tension of fighting with herself these past couple of weeks. She knocked her head back against the chair and laughed till she ached.

She wiped her eyes and looked at Sameen, who had a quizzical, half-amused look about her.

"What?" Sameen asked.

"Just...the thought of you, high on painkillers, babbling nonsense. Too much." She'd been worrying for no reason at all. And her outburst had left her so much lighter. "But don't worry, you were a perfect lady. It wasn't you, it was me. I...sort of freaked out. Things were getting a bit...you know?"

Not lies, exactly, but obscure enough.

"No, I don't know, not really. You never talk, Tara. You're such a clam. Look at this lovely house. Why have you never invited me here? And Chhaya, she's a riot."

Tara raised an eyebrow. "First-name basis already? Well, yeah, she's a riot all right." She shook her head. Suddenly, nothing seemed like a big deal anymore. She stood. "Come on, I'll show you why I've never invited you here."

Tara led Sameen to the study that was down the passage. She usually kept the door shut because the sight of the mess inside irritated her. She pushed it open and felt for the light switch on the left.

It was a spare room that doubled as a store and a study. Half the room was taken up with two Godrej cupboards that held their winter clothes, and an assortment of boxes and suitcases. The other half held a writing desk and chair, aluminium office shelves filled with files and other rubbish, and a large cloth-covered bulletin board.

Sameen glanced around at the untidy piles of printouts and the notebooks marked with Post-it notes on the desk. There was an assortment of stationery—pens, markers, pencils, thumbtacks, paper clips, files. On the bulletin board were small pieces of paper with scribbled notes accompanying an array of photographs—some rough printouts, some on photo-quality paper—mostly with Post-its stuck on them.

"Er…your mother is a private eye?" asked Sameen.

"Close. Remember those guys she keeps fixing me up with? It's much bigger than that. She's been on an intensive, long-term mission to find me a husband."

"What!"

"You heard right. And Chhaya Dixit never does anything half-heartedly. Usually, all this stuff is littered around the house, and it creeps me out. I don't know why she's tidied up. I hope it means she's found a new project. About time she did."

"What sort of project?" Sameen asked, looking dazed.

"Well, let's see." Tara closed her eyes and screwed up her forehead in an effort to recall her mother's obsessions. "There was that time she took up beekeeping, till the neighbours complained. Then there was the hairdresser phase, which was quite tame actually, which is probably why it didn't last too long. She was into ham radio when I was a kid, and weather monitoring. She's done a course in Lavani dancing. Oh, and you were almost right—she did an online private detective course. And how can I forget? She is a certified bungee-jumping instructor."

"*What?*"

"Yep. I think that was when Papa had his first heart attack." Tara shook her head. "Ever since he passed on, it's been her mission to find me a man. She's got this network of uncles and aunts reporting to her, she's on Shaadi.com, various online forums, goodness knows what else. It's been her thing for ages."

"Wow," said Sameen, blowing out her cheeks and exhaling loudly. "So…she…you mean, er, arranged marriage."

"Not exactly," said Tara. "It's just her theory that if she finds me the right guy, I'll get interested and then, who knows, maybe get married."

"Basically, she's trying to get you a boyfriend?"

Tara nodded. "Because I don't seem to be doing anything to get one myself."

Sameen stared back at Tara, her mouth open. Then she turned away and seemed to stumble. Her shoulders shook. She put her hand out to support herself on the wall.

"Sameen! Are you…"

Tears were running down Sameen's face as she waved Tara away. She was incoherent with laughter. Tara smiled with relief and then, because it was so infectious, she couldn't help cackling herself.

They laughed till their jaws and sides ached.

"Oh dear," said Sameen, wiping her eyes. "What a pity you're…not interested."

"It's a tragedy," said Tara, trying to look serious and failing.

Rohan was snoring. Usually, Sameen gave him a push and he rolled over to his side obediently and the snoring stopped. But tonight she was so lost in her own thoughts that she hardly even heard him.

Talking to Tara and clearing the air had made her feel several kilos lighter. When she'd got back home, Rohan commented about her having a spring in her step—and it was true, metaphorically, at least. Having spent two weeks wondering if Tara had been mad at her, she'd felt like skipping for joy after finding out she wasn't.

Yet something niggled at her. That look on Tara's face when she had entered the room and seen Sameen—it hadn't been surprise; it had been more like shock. Like Sameen was the last person she'd expected. And even after that, Tara had taken a good few minutes to settle down. For no reason that Sameen could figure out.

She made a mental list of the chronology of events. One, after being in and out of her house all the time, Tara had suddenly stopped coming. Two, she'd remained out of reach for a couple of weeks. Three, when Sameen had approached her, she'd seemed freaked out. Finally, they'd had a chat and dinner, and an overall nice evening, and just as suddenly everything was back to normal.

Really, Tara was lovely, but she could be *so* weird. Getting anything out of her was like squeezing blood from a stone. And

Chhaya's husband-hunting project—Sameen hadn't known whether to laugh or be shocked at first, but it had all turned out to be quite harmless. A little snigger escaped her when she thought about it. She looked quickly at Rohan, but he snored on.

Sameen pulled the covers up to her chin and smiled, thinking about how much she was looking forward to resuming their evening commute. Winter was setting in, which meant new seasonal goodies would appear on the snacking horizon.

Rohan gave an exceptionally loud snore, interrupting her daydream about carrot halwa. She gave him a nudge, and he grunted and turned over.

Chapter 13

SAMEEN WASN'T THE ONLY ONE with a spring in her step. Tara's mother commented some time the following week how much happier she looked. And Barkha remarked in her usual forthright way that the dark cloud of gloom Tara had been walking under lately seemed to have gone.

"It's like you did some serious de-stressing and detoxing," she said, frowning at her friend and then looking her up and down. She adjusted the sleeve of Tara's kurta, brushed her hair back from her forehead, and corrected the orientation of one of her earrings.

"Are you quite done, Mummy?" said Tara after waiting it out patiently.

"No, seriously. You look... Hey, are these earrings new?"

"You were with me when I bought them, two *years* ago, remember?"

"Was I?"

"Yes, now go away and let me work in peace."

Thanks to Sameen appearing unannounced at her house, Tara had been forced to admit that by forcibly cutting her out, she had only been punishing herself. And now that she'd made up her mind to set things right, that uneasy knot in her stomach was gone too.

When she thought about it, her enforced two-week space from Sameen had probably been a good thing. It had set her head back properly on her shoulders. She was an adult, she told herself. No longer an impressionable, idiotic twenty-year-old. She was in control of her emotions. Even if she was attracted to Sameen, she was hardly going to jump on her.

And in any case, the attraction had probably been a one-off thing, a momentary lapse of judgement. A dropping of boundaries after spending time in close quarters. Having spent all these years keeping her sexuality in check, she'd forgotten to acknowledge that it existed. Sure, there might have been some sparks, but Sameen was straight, so they didn't really count. And if that wasn't ice water being splashed on any developing embers, there was also the fact that Sameen was in a serious relationship, with a rather nice guy, to boot.

Most importantly, these last few days of going back to their old routine of sharing cabs and impromptu outings had made her understand one more thing. That the more time she spent with Sameen, the clearer it would become that anything romantic between them was a ridiculous, impossible idea.

After all, Tara told herself, *I'm not looking for a relationship. I'm not getting into all that drama again. And nothing can happen without my consent.*

What she did need—and want, especially from Sameen—was friendship. That was a perfectly reasonable thing to want from someone you liked, and it was stupid to let it go because of the *possibility* of being attracted to them and contemplating where that might lead. In any case, she was sure that if she had ever felt any sparks, they were well and truly extinguished now.

And the more she hung out with Sameen, the more normal things would get. They could do regular friends-type things, like talking, going out, shopping, and so on. The same kind of things she'd do with Barkha. In the unlikely event that her feelings—or rather, her madness—did resurface, she would choose not to do anything about them.

She fingered her earring. She hadn't bought herself something new in a while. She picked up her phone—Sameen was still on her speed dial.

"Hey, want to come silver shopping with me on Saturday?"

"Ooh, what's the occasion?"

"I just feel happy."

"That's great. And the reason you're happy is…?"

"Just."

Tara could hear the tapping of a keyboard in the background. "Okay," Sameen said.

"I'll buy us lunch."

"It's a date."

Something clenched inside Tara. But just for a moment. Sameen hadn't meant they go on *date* date. It was the sort of thing friends said to each other all the time.

I can do this, Tara said to herself. "A date it is."

Not doing it was not an option.

Sameen picked up the pendant and placed it on her palm. "This is so lovely." The craftwork was stunning. It was a flower with layers of petals made of fine filigree work in silver. Thin strands were drawn out and shaped in intricate patterns inside the outline of the petals.

"It is quite beautiful," Tara said.

"From Orissa, madam," said the man behind the glass-enclosed counter. "Traditional filigree work. You want to see more?"

"Yes, please." Tara examined a leaf-shaped pendant with extraordinary detail worked in with silver strands. "I love this one too," she said to Sameen. "It has matching earrings."

Sameen picked up one earring and set it against Tara's ear, brushing her hair back with the other hand. "It'll suit you. You have a long neck, and danglies look good on people with long necks."

Tara drew back, rearranging herself on the padded bench. "You should try it on too. I've never seen you wearing anything like this."

"Nah, not my thing."

"Uff, you're like Barkha—all beads and bright colours. She looks like a fruit salad sometimes."

"You think I look like a fruit salad?" asked Sameen, pretending to be offended.

"Of course not."

"Madam, do you want to see bracelets?"

Without waiting for an answer, the salesperson retreated into a back room and returned with a pile of translucent plastic boxes that he set on the counter. He removed a maroon, velvet-lined tray from under the counter and placed it before the two women. Then rooted into the plastic boxes with an air of utmost secrecy and pulled out a selection of bracelets, one by one, that he arranged on the tray.

Tara picked up a filigreed bracelet and studied it. Sameen took it from her, put it around Tara's wrist, and pushed up her sleeve so they could study it. The detailing in the design stood out against Tara's smooth brown skin.

"Wow, Tara, this looks exquisite."

Tara pulled her hand away and took a quick look at the price tag. "Aiee, no, no, just pendants for me, thank you. Or earrings. I do like the leaves."

"You should get pendants *and* earrings," Sameen said. "After all, you're celebrating feeling happy. We don't do that enough."

"Then you should get something too."

"I'm so getting this flower pendant."

Tara eventually decided on the leaf earrings and a silver owl pendant, while Sameen took the flower. It wasn't really her style of jewellery, but she was enchanted with the craftsmanship. She'd probably wear it a few times and then give it to her mother.

"I never realized you were such a silver nut," Sameen said as they left the Cottage Emporium, in search of a restaurant.

"Really? Barkha says sometimes that it seems I have silver poured on me."

"It does look good on you, though." That was true. It went well with her dusky complexion.

Sameen was famished. The salesperson had been a little sulky that his elaborate bracelet display hadn't borne any results and Sameen was sure he had packed their stuff super-slowly just to annoy them. They walked down to Saravana Bhavan in Connaught Place for lunch. It was crowded, as it always was on the weekend, but they got lucky as a table for two opened up and they were pushed up the line. They'd both set out with the intention of having dosas, but ended up ordering the set meals, along with spiced butter milk.

"I love their butter milk," Tara said, sipping her drink.

"Me too. And I'm glad we made up."

Tara looked at her for a few moments, as if mystified. "Made up?"

"You know. When you disappeared, I thought you were angry with me or something."

Tara sighed. "I'm really sorry about that. Bad decision."

Sameen grinned. "Terrible decision. Imagine what would have happened if I hadn't come chasing after you."

Tara smiled and looked away.

"Tara?"

"Yes?"

"Is…was there something else?"

"What do you mean?"

"Some other reason, I mean. Why do I feel there's something you're not telling me?"

A cloud passed over Tara's almost-black eyes. She brushed the hair away from her face and looked over Sameen's shoulder. Then her gaze returned to hold Sameen's.

"Because you have a wild imagination?" she said, one eyebrow raised.

Sameen swatted her with the menu.

Chapter 14

"WILL YOU PLEASE SIT DOWN? You're making me dizzy!"

Three long strides were all it took for Rohan to reach one side of the room from the other, and watching him go back and forth was really getting on Sameen's nerves.

"Sit down? *Sit down?*" cried Rohan. "What good will sitting down do?"

"For heaven's sake, they're just your parents," Sameen said.

"That's exactly the problem, isn't it?"

"Yes, but you're not twelve years old. You're thirty."

"Well, imagine if *your* parents were coming to visit," Rohan said, hands on hips.

"That's different."

"Why?"

"Because I've only been in Delhi for three years and you've been here since you were eighteen."

"What? That doesn't even make any sense."

Sameen flopped back on the sofa, knowing very well that her argument was flimsy. She crossed her arms. "Well, they do know about me, right?"

"Of course, that's one of the reasons they're coming."

"What!"

"Don't worry, they're not coming to marry us off. They just want to meet you."

"Yeah, right. Check out the goods, you mean?"

Rohan smirked. "And they certainly won't approve if the goods are living under the same roof as me."

Sameen threw a cushion at him.

It was no secret that more and more young people, especially young professionals who had moved away from their home towns, were living together despite disapproval from their families. In some cases, a mutually approved, don't ask, don't tell policy made sure no feathers were ruffled. When she and Rohan had got together, Sameen had casually mentioned to her parents that she had a boyfriend, patiently answered all their questions about him, and adroitly steered away any leading questions about living arrangements. Though she would never dream of telling them that she and Rohan did live together, lately she'd begun to suspect they'd figured it out.

They'd also kept each other at arm's length from their respective families because too much socializing would swiftly lead to questions about weddings, something neither of them was ready for.

"So, what? You want me to move out for ten days?" Sameen asked. "I can go stay with Milind."

"Hell, no. Then I'll have to explain to them that you live with *two* men."

"Hello, they're a couple."

But Rohan's look said it all, and Sameen held up a placating hand. "All right, all right. Why do we have to tell them who I'm staying with, though? It's not like they're coming to do a room inspection."

"You have a point." Rohan sat beside her. "So, would you?"

"It's not as simple as me packing a bag and going over. We'll have to remove all traces of my living here. Like toothbrush, make-up, all my clothes… Oh shit, you'll have to intercept my mail."

He scratched his chin. "You're right. We have to plan this carefully. You'll have to hide those little boxes, for instance." He waved a hand at a collection of lacquer boxes with miniature art on them. "My parents will never believe that I would have stuff like that."

"But they'll believe you have three kinds of non-stick cookware?"

"Oh, the books. Please hide your Mills and Boons."

"No way!"

"What if they think *I* read them?"

"I'm having to move out of my own house, so you can handle a few MBs." Sameen pursed her lips, which meant that was the end of that discussion.

She flounced off into the kitchen and filled the kettle for some tea. Rohan was right. It was always going to be a problem if any one of their parents ever decided to come for a visit—and it was something they'd discussed before. But even then, Sameen felt irritated. She hated packing. Unpacking was even worse.

And ten days of not seeing Tara.

That thought took her unawares. Somehow, their daily conversations and commutes had become part of Sameen's routine. Without Tara, her day was incomplete.

She sighed as she took out mugs and put in sugar and teabags. Maybe it wouldn't be so bad. *It'll give me a chance to hang out with Milind.*

But that thought didn't bring her any joy. In fact, it just underscored how much more she'd miss Tara. Milind was great, but he was no Tara. Sameen wondered what it was about her that made everything and everyone fade in comparison, sometimes even Rohan. She wished they could continue meeting every day. Perhaps she should talk to Tara to figure out a plan.

Tara joined the others in staring at the pile of flattened cardboard cartons. "You're moving?"

Her tone was incredulous, but the lack of any urgency from Sameen, Rohan, and Milind suggested that something else was up. Also, there was Sameen—with a large hanky around her hair and brandishing, for unspecified reasons, a feather duster, like one of those women from the retro magazine ads for household goods. Tara suppressed a smile at how charming she looked.

"Temporarily," Sameen said breezily. "I'm going to pretend I don't live here while Rohan's parents are visiting."

"Ah, I see." Relief washed over Tara. She took out her phone. "I have to take a photo of you looking like this."

Sameen waved the duster at her and struck up a pose. Tara laughed. "This is going on my Instagram. So where are you going to live?"

"At my place," Milind said.

"Oh." Tara's heart fell at the thought of Sameen being more than a two-minute walk away. "For how long?"

"Ten days," Sameen said, grimacing. She stuck out her lower lip in exaggeration. "Who's going to pick me up from office now and feed me momos?"

"Not me," Milind put in. "You can get your own momos."

"Wait a minute." Tara looked around at all of them. "Why don't you come and stay with me, Sameen?"

Rohan, who was making boxes from the flat packs, stopped. "Actually, that's a really good idea. It'll be so much easier—we could just carry the stuff across. Are you sure it's not a problem, Tara? It's *ten* days."

"Of course not. My mother's a little crazy sometimes, but Sameen knows that."

"Oh, come on, Chhaya's lovely." Sameen gave Tara a one-armed hug and left her arm around her. "You're sure?"

"Absolutely." Tara could feel the warmth of Sameen's hand through her T-shirt and the way her arm curved across her back. When Sameen took her arm away, Tara's skin still tingled. *Stop it!* Tara told herself sternly. She felt warm, much warmer than the cool evening warranted, and her heart beat just that bit faster.

That was when she realized she'd made a big mistake. How would she live with Sameen under the same roof for so many days? How would she go to sleep knowing that Sameen was in the next room? How would she share her bathroom with Sameen without imagining her...er... *Let's not go there!*

She was already losing her mind and Sameen hadn't even moved in yet.

Could she rescind the offer? No, that would just seem strange. There was nothing she could do about it now.

With a start, she noticed that Milind was looking at her with his head cocked to one side, eyes questioning. Tara's face burned. She blinked and looked away.

"Well?" asked Milind.

"Oh, er...what?"

"I asked if it would be okay to take a few things over tonight. Since I have my car."

"R-right, sure. I'll just call Mama and give her a heads-up."

"What are you going to tell her?" Rohan sounded worried.

Sameen gave him a little push. "The truth, silly."

"But…"

"Oh, she'll be fine with it, I know she will," Tara said.

"Cool." Rohan rubbed his hands together. He seemed relieved. "Thanks, Tara."

"You're very welcome. So…we have, what, three days before they arrive? What do we need to do?"

Sameen picked up her phone from the table and called up a list she'd made. She read it out to Tara. "Can you think of anything else?"

Tara gave it a thought. "Well, you'll have to tell your cleaning person to not ask pointed questions."

Rohan blanched. "Shit!" He sat down heavily.

"Relax," Milind said, slapping his back. "We have three days. We'll figure it all out."

Tara caught Sameen's eye and gave her a half-smile. Sameen smiled back. "We shall have lots of fun, won't we?"

"We shall have to find something else to binge-watch," Tara said. A frisson of anxiety surged through her.

Ten whole days, just her and Sameen.

She was so screwed.

Chapter 15

BARKHA AND HER HUSBAND KUNAL lived in a beautiful two-storey house, a refurbished colonial bungalow, with a spacious lawn bordered with flowerbeds, in Jangpura Extension. The perimeter wall was densely covered with creepers, making it impossible to tell what lay beneath. A gulmohar tree stood stoutly at the corner, which doubtless covered the lawn—and the neighbours'—with orange blossoms during summer.

"It was nice of Barkha to invite me," Sameen said, hooking her arm around Tara's as they headed towards the door.

"I would have brought you even if she hadn't." Tara slipped her arm out of Sameen's as she reached for the door. "After all, I couldn't leave my guest alone the very first night, could I? What with Mama deciding on her last-minute trip too."

There must have been about a hundred guests inside, with black-and-white-clad servers weaving between them, carting drinks and snacks around. Tall French doors from the living room led to a shaded patio that stepped down to the lawn. The doors had been thrown open and the party had spilled outside. Fairy lights were strung on bushes, looking like little stars shining out of the darkness.

"Wow," Sameen said as Tara led her inside. "What does Kunal do?"

"He owns a couple of fancy restaurants. Swanky house, isn't it? Come on, I'll introduce you."

Kunal, Tara had told her, had a reputation for throwing blowout parties, so Sameen was rather mystified to be introduced to a small, shy man, nervously looking around from behind a pair of glasses. He didn't say much, either, just thanked them for coming and then scurried off. The next time Sameen saw him, he was behind the bar, shaking a cocktail for someone.

"He's a bit of a contradiction." Tara's voice in her ear made her jump.

"Er...what?"

Tara grinned. "I noticed you've been watching him and you look a bit puzzled. He's incredibly funny and friendly if you meet him one-on-one, but he seems to go into his shell in a crowd. But he *loves* to play host."

Barkha floated by, outfitted in a body-hugging, shimmering, black-and-silver salwar suit, looking like something out of a fashion magazine. Tara caught her arm and pulled her over. "You look stunning."

Barkha patted the carefully arranged pile of glittering ringlets at the side of her head, and gave a lopsided grin. "Yeah, I do, don't I? Hi, Sameen, thanks for coming."

"Thanks for inviting me." Sameen handed her a small gift-wrapped box. "And congratulations."

"Thank you," she said graciously. "Ten years definitely deserves *some* congratulations, no?"

"Ten years?" Sameen asked. "You must have married when you were...what, thirteen?"

"Ha ha, flatterer." Barkha gave her arm a friendly slap. "You're welcome back here anytime." She winked at Sameen and melted away into the crowd.

"They married straight out of college," said Tara. "Both twenty-one. If I had a rupee for all the lying and covering I did for her while they were romancing," she sighed, "I'd probably have a place as grand as this one."

A large group from Tara and Barkha's work swept up and pulled Tara away with them. Sameen wandered around the room, admiring the decor and the expensive artwork on the walls. She walked out into the hall and studied the wall of photos—all in black wooden frames, arranged in a group, like a collage. They were all of Barkha and Kunal, with families, with friends, on holidays. She was surprised to see baby photos too, Barkha and Kunal with growing kids, the latest showing them to be around six or seven. She made a note to ask Tara about them—she hadn't known Barkha had children.

Somewhat bored, Sameen walked to the French doors and stepped outside. A server came by with a tray of wine, and she got rid of her empty glass and picked up another white wine. It was a cool December evening. Winter had yet to set in properly, and being outside was still pleasant. She sat on a wrought-iron bench on the patio. Another server appeared with mushroom-and-cheese quiches, and Sameen snagged a few.

She spotted Tara and Barkha with the group from their office out on the lawn. Barkha was talking and gesturing, while the others were laughing at whatever story she was telling. Tara smacked Barkha's shoulder playfully, then threw her head back and laughed, the sound carrying to Sameen. She smiled. Seeing Tara let her hair down for a change was nice—she was usually so intense.

Tara had on a simple brown tussar silk kurta with black piping along the neck and sleeves, paired with a rich maroon churidar. A maroon dupatta speckled with silvery bits hung over one shoulder. She was also wearing the silver leaf earrings they had bought together at the Cottage Emporium. A small pendant with a blood-red stone on a chain hung in the hollow of her neck. The light fell on Tara's hair, making it shine like it was polished. She brushed a strand from her face and tucked it behind her ear. Her finger was tapping restlessly on the glass she held with both hands. Her face was in shadow, but Sameen pictured it as being flushed and happy. The strand of hair she had brushed away fell loose again. Sameen imagined brushing it gently back behind her ear again. She could almost feel the warmth of Tara's skin. Her fingertips tingled, a quiver passing down her whole body.

She jumped when a hoarse voice spoke next to her. "Madam, mutton shami kabab?" It was only one of the penguin-suited servers. She shook her head and he went away. When she turned back to where Tara had been, she was gone.

Sameen leaned back against the bench, overcome by a peculiar sense of melancholy tinged with a sort of happy excitement. She couldn't understand it—she wasn't sad, but tears filled her eyes. Yet she felt so happy that her heart seemed too big for her chest.

Tara piled half a dozen fish fingers on a paper napkin and shouldered through the crowd, smiling and nodding at familiar faces. She had seen Sameen sitting on the bench outside, looking rather out of place, and had felt a twinge of guilt. Sameen was still there, sipping from a glass of wine.

"Fish fingers, madam?" she said in an imitation of the servers.

Sameen smiled. "There you are."

Tara plopped down next to her. "Sorry for abandoning you."

"Don't be. I'm okay."

"I forgot you don't know anyone."

"Yes, but you know everyone, so you shouldn't have to hang out with me."

"Oh, shut up and eat your fish fingers. Wait, hang on to these, I want to get a drink. You want something?"

"No, I'm good."

Kunal, who was playing bartender as usual to get out of heavy-duty socializing, recommended a new single-malt whisky he'd just acquired. "Just for you," he said, shooting her a conspiratorial look as he poured a generous measure over ice. "How's your friend?"

"Tucking into snacks."

Indeed, by the time Tara got back, Sameen had polished off all the fish fingers. "Sorry—I was hungry. Shall I get you more?"

"It's okay," Tara said, laughing. "We'll just intercept the waiter when he goes by. Cheers."

"Cheers." Sameen raised her glass and they clinked them together. "You know, in Germany—or is it France?—they say you must look into each other's eyes while toasting or..."

"Or what?" Tara asked.

"Erm, it's seven years of bad sex."

"Oh." Tara didn't know what else to say. She was disconcerted to find that her face was growing warm. Small mercies for being too dark to blush. She forced a laugh. "Well, we wouldn't want that, would we? Let's toast again."

They did so, giggling like teenagers. But Tara wondered what good it would do her. It wasn't like women were lining up at her bedroom door.

Servers passed with an assortment of snacks, which they tucked into with abandon. Someone turned up the music inside, and Tara could almost feel the walls shaking.

"Is your purse vibrating?" Tara pointed out after a bit.

Sameen scrabbled about in her purse that was lying between them and retrieved her phone. Rohan's grinning face, wearing a woollen hat with two braids, was lit up on the screen. The missed-call icon was also visible at the top. Sameen answered, putting a finger in her other ear. "Hi, Ro, what's up? ... What? I can't hear you. It's too noisy."

Tara tapped her shoulder and beckoned her to follow. She led Sameen around the side of the house to the back, where the noise dropped to a low hubbub of voices and the gentle thrum of bass.

"Yes, I can hear now. What's up?" Sameen asked. She listened for a couple of seconds and her face moulded into a frown.

"At Barkha's anniversary party ... Tara's friend. I told you ... Yeah, sorry, didn't hear your calls. Is everything okay?"

From the way Sameen tensed, Tara could tell this wasn't a happy conversation. She gestured to Sameen that she was going back to the house and retreated, as Sameen said, "You can't make last-minute plans and expect me..."

Tara ran the last few steps around the corner so she didn't hear what Rohan had expected Sameen to do. She waited for a few minutes and, when Sameen didn't turn up, she ventured back to see if she was okay.

Sameen was off the phone, sitting on a stone bench by the wall. She leaned forward, her head in her hands.

"Hey," Tara called. "Everything all right?"

Sameen looked up. "Yeah, yeah, just dandy," she said with a sigh, moving over to let Tara sit next to her. "Apparently, Rohan made plans to go out for dinner with his parents and said I would join them, and now he's pissed because I can't."

"But he knew you were coming here with me."

"Yeah, but he forgot."

"Why are *you* upset? He's the one who mixed up the dates."

"I know, just…"

"Just what?"

"He…he seemed really tense. I don't know why. I don't know why it's such a big deal." She caught Tara's hand. "Tara, I'm so afraid that…that…"

Sameen's hand was chilled. Tara put her other hand on top of hers and held tight. "What are you afraid of, Sameen?" she asked gently.

"That it's just like we thought. That his parents are here to check me out, as wife material, you know."

A numbing sense of disappointment settled within Tara. She swallowed. "And that's a bad thing?"

"No, yes, I don't know! I don't want to think of getting married right now." She looked around, then laughed softly. "What an irony, talking about all this here."

Tara smiled. "Yeah. But you and Rohan… I thought you were serious."

"We are, but we're also on the same page about not getting married for a few years. At least I thought we were."

Tara didn't respond. What would it be like if Sameen did marry Rohan? The thought opened a raw wound inside her. She couldn't help it. She knew Sameen was her friend—her straight friend—but still.

Chapter 16

TARA ROLLED HER CHAIR TO Barkha's cubicle and they sat, side by side, to have their lunch.

"Egg curry and rice today, yum." Barkha waved to the lunch boy. "Vivek, do you have any green chillies? Oh, thank you."

Tara ripped open her container of curd and spooned some on to her rice. The chillies were usually pretty deadly, and it helped to have something to neutralize them with.

"So," Barkha began, "Sameen still staying with you?"

"Mmhm," mumbled Tara, her mouth full.

One of the other writers on their team, Mike, popped his head over the cubicle. "Hey, Tara, what are the chances you'll swap my Bengal Football League coverage with the T20 tournament in January?"

"Zero," replied Tara amiably.

"Can I bribe you?"

"Sure. Buy me a Merc?"

"Aww." He made a sad face and sat back down.

"So," Barkha said when he was gone, "I have to ask, is there anything going on between you and Sameen?"

Some of her food went down the wrong way and Tara coughed. Barkha patted her on the back and pushed a bottle of water towards her. Tara waved it away and swallowed.

"Are you *insane?*" she asked.

Barkha sliced a small piece off her boiled egg and carefully placed it on top of a mound of rice, then spooned the whole thing into her mouth. As she chewed, she looked up at Tara. She swallowed her mouthful and said, "Are you sure?"

"Yes, I'm *sure,*" Tara said. "Whatever makes you think... Oh god, you're so impossible!"

"She's in a relationship, Tara," Barkha warned.

"You're not *listening* to me," Tara said through gritted teeth. "There's *nothing* going on. And anyway, she's *straight*. With a *boyfriend*, and it's *serious*."

Barkha played around with her food. "Just that...that night, at the party, the way she was looking at you..."

"What do you mean looking at me?" Tara demanded. Outraged though she was, Barkha's statement intrigued her. "Looking at me how?"

"All intense and...I don't know. It just seemed..."

"Seemed what?"

"I don't know. That night, you two had eyes only for each other."

"She didn't know anyone there. Of course I had to hang around with her."

Barkha pursed her lips. "Look, I don't know about her, but you... I don't want you to get hurt."

"I'm not going to get hurt. Because there's nothing happening, okay?"

"Maybe you're too close to her and you can't see it, but please be careful."

"Will you stop it?" Tara snapped. "Nothing will happen. I won't let it. You know I haven't since Radhika."

"Yeah, about that. Sometimes we fall for people. We can't help it. It's not always in our control."

"Yes, it is. It's in mine. Everyone is not flaky like you." Tara's face was hot with anger. She picked up her plate and curd container, shoved back her chair, and stalked off to her own cubicle. Only once she got there did she realize that her chair was back at Barkha's desk.

Tara left her food and went to the bathroom. She locked herself in a stall and stood before the toilet, staring down with unseeing eyes. She was shaking. She stood there for a long time. The blood was ringing in her head.

What if Barkha is right?

Being around Sameen made her happy. It made her feel good, uplifted. It made her feel that the world was a better place. It made her want to make other people happy. Was that a bad thing? Yes, she could admit she was attracted to Sameen. But that didn't mean she was falling for her, did it?

Did it? she asked herself.

A door squeaked open, and voices and laughter filled the room as someone talked about their new iPhone.

No, it didn't. I'm not going to let it happen. All other complications aside, she's straight.

Her resolve back in place, Tara left the stall and went to the sink. She splashed some water on her face before checking herself in the mirror and walking out.

Her half-eaten lunch was cold and the sight of it nauseated her. Her chair was back in its place and a small Dairy Milk chocolate lay next to her computer.

"What's wrong? You've been aloof all weekend," Rohan said. "Don't you like my parents?"

"Your parents are great," Sameen replied, staring at the pile of old travel magazines on the table in front of them. Tara had been betting that either travel or bringing out a magazine about it would be her mother's upcoming fad. "It's you I have a problem with."

"What do you mean?"

"I'm waiting for an apology."

"What am I supposed to have done?"

"Supposed to have done? You were a complete ass that evening, Rohan. You knew I'd be at the party with Tara."

Rohan groaned. "Oh, that again. Come on, I forgot, I told you. It's no big deal."

"It is a big deal. You can't assume I'm just going to hang around waiting for an invitation from you."

"My parents had just arrived that morning. They wanted to meet you. What was I supposed to do?"

"Tell them I had plans?"

"I told you, I forgot. They're here for the first time. When have I ever asked you for something like this?"

"Doesn't matter. You can't do this to me. Assume I can drop everything and come running."

"All right, all right. Can we let it go? Will you come with us to the Sound and Light Show at the Red Fort tomorrow night?"

"I'll come if you apologize."

"Okay, yaar, I'm sorry," Rohan said, placing a hand on Sameen's thigh. "I shouldn't have assumed you're sitting around, twiddling your thumbs, waiting for me to call."

There was a click and creak of the door opening. Sameen shifted her leg away from Rohan. Tara walked in a moment later, and her eyebrows rose when she saw them. "Oh, hello."

She dropped her bag on the dining table and went into the kitchen. Sameen heard water running, and pots and pans banging around. Rohan got up.

"I should go," he said. "I told them I was out for a walk."

"Okay, see you tomorrow, then."

"We're okay?"

"Yeah, we're fine." She gave him a friendly shove. "Off you go now."

After he left, Sameen went looking for Tara. She was still in the kitchen, chopping vegetables with undue violence.

"Can I help?" asked Sameen.

"You could wash some rice," Tara replied without looking up. "It's in that cupboard."

Sameen measured some out into a pan. There was something about Tara—a sort of warning signal coming off her in waves. "Are you all right?"

"Yeah, I'm fine," Tara said shortly.

Sameen stared at the back of her head as Tara slammed the lid on the pressure cooker and turned on the burner.

"Are you upset about Rohan hanging out here?" she asked.

She looked up. "What? Of course not."

Then she went into the bathroom, banging the door shut.

Sameen bit her lip, wondering what was wrong. She set the rice to cook on the other burner and turned the flame down. Then she went out into the living room and sat before the TV, surfing aimlessly.

Tara came out ten minutes later in a pair of track pants and an oversized sweatshirt, hair wet from a shower. "I'm sorry I was grumpy," she said. "Had a really bad day at work."

Sameen grimaced in sympathy. "Rohan and I sort of had a fight. But I think we made up."

Tara came and sat next to her. Her towel was spread across her shoulders and there was a damp patch where water from her hair had dripped.

"Want to talk about it?" Sameen asked.

"Nah, not really. You?"

"Nope. It's sorted."

Tara nodded. "What are you watching?"

"Nothing. Channel-surfing. There's nothing to watch, as usual."

"We could stream something."

"I guess." Sameen grinned. "Unless…"

"What?" Tara narrowed her eyes.

"Want to binge-watch one of my all-time favourite TV series? It's about two women, a mother-and-daughter pair. *Gilmore Girls*."

"Oh yeah, I've heard about it. Used to come on TV when I was a kid."

"It's got the cutest romance between Lorelai, the mother, and the town's diner owner, Luke, who—"

Tara interrupted her with a raised hand. "Hang on, do you want me to watch it or are you going to tell me the whole story right now?"

Sameen beamed. "I have it on my laptop. Do you have an HDMI cable?"

"In my room."

"Good, good. Hey, I forgot to ask, did Chhaya call? Has she reached—"

"Oh, yes she has. She said hello and instructed me to feed you properly."

On cue, the pressure cooker whistled. "Damn, I'd forgotten about that." Tara got up again and padded to the kitchen. "Oh good, you did the rice," she called to Sameen.

Sameen followed Tara and watched her turn off the burner and drain the excess water from the rice into the sink.

"It's sort of unfair that you have to cook," she said. "Maybe I can make something tomorrow."

Tara looked over her shoulder at Sameen. "That means we're having tea and toast for dinner, right?"

"Well, I can also make boiled potatoes and jam sandwiches."

Tara's horrified expression made Sameen laugh.

"No thanks," Tara said. "I am rather fond of my dinner, and I like real food."

"But I destroy any *real* food I try to cook."

Tara inclined her head and studied Sameen. "Maybe I can teach you a few things."

"My dear, braver souls have tried and failed to teach me to cook. I'm banned from touching Rohan's special pressure cooker and his ceramic non-stick pan set. And I don't even know which one that is."

"That's because Rohan is a control freak in the kitchen."

Sameen narrowed her eyes. "Yeah, you're right. Okay, you may have a go."

"Great, we shall start tomorrow."

"Not tomorrow. I'm going to Red Fort with his parents."

"Oh, okay. The day after, then. Right, dinner will be ready in about ten minutes—dal with vegetables, and rice."

"Super. I shall set up *Gilmore Girls*, then."

Chapter 17

"ALL RIGHT," TARA SAID, HANDING Sameen an apron, which she reluctantly pulled on. "Today, we're going to teach you how to make egg curry and chapatis."

"Ooh, lovely." Sameen rubbed her hands together. "Egg curry is my favourite and I already know how to boil eggs."

Tara took the lid off a pan sitting on the burner. "The eggs are already boiled."

Sameen pouted. "Not fair."

Tara smacked her hand lightly with a wooden spoon. "No talking back."

"Yes, ma'am."

As she turned away to the refrigerator, Sameen stuck a tongue out at her. "Hey, I saw that. Now what do you think egg curry is made of?"

Sameen screwed up her eyes in thought. "Um...well, there's eggs, of course. Water, salt, um, turmeric?"

"Do you remember what we used for the chicken curry the other day?" asked Tara.

"Yes. There were onions, tomatoes, and ginger-garlic paste. And dry spices."

"Yes, very good. Now, do you want to chop the onions while I do the other stuff?"

"Okay."

Sameen picked up the knife and carefully started peeling an onion. "Tara?"

"Hmm?"

"Why are we doing this?"

"Onions are an important ingredient in egg curries."

"That's not what I mean."

"Then what do you mean?"

"I have a boyfriend who loves to cook for me every day, so why am I torturing myself like this?" Sameen gestured to the tears streaming down her cheeks.

"What will happen if he's not around to cook for you?"

"But you will always be there, won't you?" Sameen's eyes had a playful gleam.

Tara's heart raced. She stared into the hypnotizing eyes that were waiting for a response from her. "Always," Tara heard herself saying before the spell broke.

"So does that mean I can stop?"

"No! Get that finished quickly." She pointed at the chopping board. "You still have to cut the tomatoes."

"Tyrant," Sameen muttered. She sniffed as she wiped her eyes on her sleeve. "Where did you learn how to cook?"

"From my father. He was a chef."

"Oh really? Rohan would've loved to meet him." Sameen put the onions into a bowl and moved the tomatoes to the chopping board. "So would I. Were you close?"

"Yeah…" Tara felt that pang in her heart that she always did whenever she thought of her father. "He used to work odd hours, so most days we wouldn't see each other at home. Some days he would pick me up from school and take me with him to the restaurant. I would spend hours there playing with him. Cooking and food were a big part of our games. Even now, every time I enter the kitchen, I think of him."

"My dad can't cook to save his life," Sameen said.

"Like father, like daughter?" Tara raised her eyebrow.

"Totally."

They grinned at each other.

"Done," Sameen said finally.

"Go wash your eyes. You're a mess."

When she came back, under Tara's guidance, Sameen set up the pan, heated the oil, and soon the spices were simmering away. Sameen suddenly had a bout of sneezing.

"Wow. These masalas are strong."

"That's what cooking is all about, my dear. Come, we shall now knead the dough for the chapatis." Tara told Sameen how to measure out the flour and how to get the dough's consistency right. The doorbell rang as they were getting out the flour.

"Back in a minute. It must be a courier."

When Tara came returned, she stopped at the kitchen door and watched Sameen struggle with the dough. Her fingers were coated with clumps of wholewheat flour. Rivulets of water ran along the sides of the flat dish she had been kneading in. Her hair and face were streaked with white. Sameen had never looked so endearing.

Tara sighed, then shook her head and went to stand next to Sameen. Without thinking what she was doing, she placed her hand over Sameen's and plunged it into the gooey mess. "You can't be squeamish about this. You have to literally get your hands dirty," she said quietly. "You keep pressing it together like this, gathering the loose flour from the sides. When it starts to come together, it'll stop sticking to your hand."

Their fingers were intertwined as their hands moved as one. Tara noticed how soft Sameen's hand was despite the coating of dough. Sameen turned to look at her, and Tara caught her gaze and smiled. "It'll work, you'll see."

"I think you're nuts," she said, but she was smiling too. Then she closed her eyes and turned her head slightly, as if thinking. "You know, I never thought gooey messes could feel kind of good."

The smell of Sameen's herbal shampoo was in Tara's nose and she felt an undeniable thrill at having her fingers laced with Sameen's inside a soft, warm lump of dough. "It does, doesn't it?"

Sameen opened her eyes and smiled at Tara. Tara smiled back. Their arms crossed one another's, and she realized with a sudden jolt that they'd stopped kneading.

Tara's face flamed as she pulled her hand out. The acrid smell of burning masalas filled the kitchen.

"Shit, the spices are burnt!" Tara ran towards the burner and turned off the gas. Right then, the key clicked in the lock and her mother's voice filled the house. "Tara? What's burning?"

"Nothing, Mama." She dumped the pan in the sink and rushed out to greet her, heart still thudding. "You're back early. Here, let me take your bag. Are you hungry? Can I get you some water?"

"What's the matter? Are you okay?" Her mother asked, looking Tara up and down. She relinquished her bag and sat herself down on the chair Tara had pulled out from the dining table. "You look like you've seen a ghost. You did know I was returning today, didn't you?"

"Yes, yes, of course. Just... How are you, Mama?"

"I'm very well. I just spoke to you this morning. Are you sure you're okay?"

Tara pushed the hair back from her forehead, blinking. *Was she okay?*

"What's that white stuff in your hair?" her mother asked.

By the time Tara returned to the kitchen after sending her mother off to freshen up, she had collected herself. Sameen was staring desperately at a fresh pile of onions and tomatoes, knife in hand. But at least she'd managed to clean up.

"Oh wow, Sameen Siddiqi, you *are* completely useless in the kitchen," said Tara, forcing herself to sound casual.

"Umm, sorry?" Sameen said, looking anything but. "But it's your fault. I warned you."

Tara rolled her eyes. "Come on, let's fix this."

They worked companionably side by side, Tara doing all the chopping, frying, roasting, and stirring, while Sameen peered over her shoulder, trying to look helpful.

"Shall I make a salad?" she asked. "I can do that without disaster."

"Disaster? What disaster?" Tara said innocently. "We have been such good girls."

"What smells so good?" asked Tara's mother, standing at the kitchen door. "Sameen, is she making you cook? Tara, how can you make the guest cook?"

Tara laughed and went over to give her mother a hug. "Sameen has made her special egg curry for us, Mama," she said as she winked at Sameen, who averted her gaze for a moment and then smiled.

Tara poured the egg curry into a serving dish, thinking about how having Sameen to stay hadn't been the unmitigated disaster she'd feared. In fact, it had been pleasant, fun even. She sprinkled fresh coriander leaves on the egg curry, and admitted to herself that she might even miss Sameen when she moved back, even though in some ways it would be a relief.

Tara watched her mother and Sameen engaged in an animated conversation as they set the table in the dining area. She felt a sudden hollowness.

What if she didn't have to keep holding back all the time?

The thought jerked her back to reality. *Wow, where did that come from?*

Sameen looked at the phone on her lap for the umpteenth time, making sure the people sitting around the table hadn't noticed. This had to be the longest lunch of her life. Rohan's parents had invited her to a fancy restaurant that served the best Italian cuisine in the city, but the conversation had been mind-numbing.

Five minutes after arriving at the restaurant, she had realized she didn't have anything to contribute to the discussion that Rohan's parents were steering. It was all about money, business, property, the stock market, and more money. She had tuned out ages ago, and hoped she was smiling and nodding in all the right places.

"What do you think, Sameen?"

She was startled out of her languor to find three sets of eyes looking at her expectantly.

"Um…" she said, having no clue who had asked the question and, worse, what that question was. She slowly picked up the glass of water in front of her and took a sip to buy herself some time when her phone rang. Relief washed over her, which was immediately replaced with joy as Tara's face lit up her phone.

"Excuse me, I have to take this," she said as she got up from her chair and headed towards the door.

"Your timing is impeccable," Sameen said when she stepped out of the restaurant.

"I take it lunch is not going well?" Tara asked.

"I think I would have more fun dead."

"Ouch."

"Yeah. You have no idea how happy I am to hear your voice. You just saved me from the most embarrassing moment of my life."

"Always glad to be of service."

Sameen smiled. Tara had been her saviour once again. She was losing count of the number of times her friend had bailed her out. She always knew when Sameen needed her most and exactly what that need was. Sameen had never shared such a deep connection with any of her friends, and she knew now what a big void Tara's presence filled in her life.

"I was calling to ask if you'd like to go out tomorrow evening," Tara continued. "You know they are shutting down Regal in a few months, right?"

"Ah yes, the oldest and famous-est movie theatre in the city that all you Delhi-ites are so proud of?"

"Yes. That theatre was such a big part of my childhood. My parents and I watched many movies there. They're having a Raj Kapoor retrospective at the moment. I wondered if you'd like to come and see *Mera Naam Joker* with me tomorrow."

"Of course I'll come with you," Sameen said. The thought of an outing with Tara filled her with happiness.

"Great. Thanks," Tara said. "I'll let you get back to your lunch."

"Ugh. I'll see you at home if I survive."

Chapter 18

THE ENTRANCE TO REGAL CINEMA was packed. People jostled each other in long queues at the ticket counter, trying to figure out if they could still buy tickets, the prominently displayed board that had "House Full" painted on it in bold letters notwithstanding. The white walls of the building were decorated with colourful posters from Raj Kapoor's films, in front of which many people were taking selfies and videos.

Tara stood still, studying the crowd as she mentally mapped a route through it towards the lobby. Just then she heard Sameen's voice in her ear.

"Wow. I'm so glad you bought the tickets in advance. We would've never got any here."

"I owe a lot of people a lot of favours," Tara said. "Come on."

Without another thought, she grabbed Sameen's hand and led them towards the lobby, following the mental map she'd just made. She only became aware of what she'd done when the warmth and softness of Sameen's hand in hers sent waves of pleasure through her arm. Conflicting feelings warred within her—should she hold on or let go? Before she could find a solution, they had entered the calmer and quieter lobby, and Tara dropped her hand like it was a bomb.

"Um, do you want popcorn or something?" Tara asked, fidgeting with the strap of her handbag.

"Of course. But let me take care of that. You go grab our seats and I'll meet you inside."

"Okay," she said, handing Sameen her ticket.

Tara found her seat and plonked herself in it, taking a few deep breaths. How could such an innocent contact take her breath away like this?

Enough, she told herself.

The seats she had managed to get were in the first row in the balcony, from where the entire layout of the theatre was visible. She put her arms on the balustrade and peered at the lower stall. It looked quite run-down. The front stall seats, which were all bent at odd angles, had nails and screws poking out from various joints. The blue-and-white paint on the walls was chipping and there was a big patch of water seepage in one corner. The floor also needed repairing. The only things that had retained their charm were the colonial-style arches spread all along the left and right of the hall. Perhaps it wasn't such a bad thing that the place was being renovated.

"Feeling nostalgic about your childhood?" Sameen asked as she handed Tara a Coke and settled into the seat on her right.

"Not really. This place can definitely do with a bit of serious sprucing up," Tara said as she straightened in her seat.

"Ah, they're dimming the lights," Sameen said, turning towards the screen. "You know, I've never seen this film before. It's such a classic; I don't know how I've missed watching it."

Tara looked at Sameen. She was transfixed by the way the light from the screen made Sameen's face glimmer. Her nerve endings felt like they were on high alert. She was hyperaware of Sameen's every movement, the smell of her perfume, the rise and fall of her chest.

Tara was struggling to bring her focus back to the movie when Sameen gently touched her arm as she whispered, "That's Rishi Kapoor, isn't it? He must have barely been sixteen when he acted in this."

The warmth of Sameen's hand on her arm and her breath caressing Tara's ear caused shivers to run down Tara's body, to places she didn't even know existed. She had no idea what was going on in the film, even though she'd seen it a few times before. She was even struggling to remember what Sameen had said.

"Huh? Um…yeah…it is…" Tara cleared her throat. "It was his…er…first film," she somehow managed to get out.

Sameen moved her hand away, and Tara breathed a sigh of relief.

This was not good.

"Home!" cried Sameen, letting her suitcase go, which fell over with a thump on the floor. She flopped on the sofa, spreading her arms and legs wide to take up the entire space. "Oh, I missed you so much."

"I missed you too," Rohan said, trying to squeeze in beside her.

"I don't mean you, silly. I was talking to the sofa."

"You know what, I don't even care right now. I love my parents, but I'm so happy to get my home back." Rohan let his head fall back against the sofa. "Oh, I feel ten kilos lighter."

"Was it really awful, having your parents here?" Sameen asked.

"Well, it was weird. They sort of took over—my mum cooked and managed the house, my dad got provisions and stuff. It was like I was a little boy again. They paid for everything. They didn't seem to get the fact that I've been living on my own for years now and I can look after myself."

"Yeah, well, parents. They can be clueless like that." Sameen leaned on Rohan's shoulder. "I'm happy to be back too."

"Was it really terrible at Tara's, then? Did she give you only dry bread and water?"

"Oh, it was just ghastly," Sameen said. "I slept in a cupboard under the stairs."

"Guess what, you can have your very own bed now."

"My very own? But where will you sleep?"

"Hmm…bathroom mat?"

"Okay, sounds fair."

They sat lazily in silence for a while. Sameen looked around the room. It was good to be home, but truth be told, she would miss Tara quite a bit. She would miss their late-night chats and their marathon TV series sessions. Not to mention getting up late the next day, bleary-eyed and rushing about to make it to work on time. She would even miss dividing up the daily chores—at least till Chhaya had come back and been appalled that Tara had been making her work. Her heart sank at thinking there would be no more midnight hot chocolates or stretching out on the carpet under blankets in front of the TV.

Rohan broke the silence. "What are you thinking?"

"Nothing," Sameen said, feeling a little guilty. "Just that I had fun staying with Tara."

"But I'm your favourite roomie, no?" he said, putting his arm around her.

"Yup," Sameen replied automatically. "Of course."

Rohan moved closer and Sameen closed her eyes as their lips touched. She allowed the kiss to deepen, realizing it had been quite a while and she'd missed this too.

"Hey, Sameen, you forgot—"

They sprang apart. Sameen turned towards the door and froze. Tara was standing there with a small bag in her hand.

"Oh, sorry. I-I just…" Tara began, looking around everywhere but at them. "I'll see you later." She dumped the bag on the floor and turned.

"Tara, don't go." Rohan jumped up from the sofa and walked towards her. "Come on in. I was just going to open some wine. Will you join us?"

"I-I don't want to disturb you. Also, I have some work to take care of."

"You're not disturbing us. Stay for one drink. I haven't had the chance to properly thank you for taking such good care of my girlfriend. Sameen, you ask her. She'll stay if you ask."

Sameen blinked at Rohan. She was still on the sofa, not trusting her legs to hold her if she stood, though she wasn't sure why. She was also having a tough time looking at Tara, but she knew both of them were waiting for her to say something. She looked away from Rohan and forced herself to meet Tara's eyes.

"Stay," she said softly.

Tara looked at her, an unfamiliar expression on her face.

"Please," Sameen said, no longer able to hold Tara's gaze. From the corner of her vision, she saw Tara nod.

"Okay."

"Great." Rohan grinned and went into the kitchen.

An awkward silence descended on the room.

"Um, sit," Sameen said, looking at Tara's shoulder.

"Huh? Oh yeah," replied Tara and came over and sat on the chair next to the sofa. The silence between them was unbearable. Sameen desperately looked for something to say, but words were completely failing her.

"So the house is yours again? You must be so glad to be back home," Tara said to the coffee table.

"Y-yeah."

"So when are *your* parents coming over?"

"Not anytime soon. I'll be visiting them early next year. My cousin's getting married."

"Oh, nice."

Rohan returned with three glasses and a bottle of wine, and placed them on the table. He filled the glasses and handed them out to Tara and Sameen simultaneously.

"Here you are, ladies." He sat down and put his free arm around Sameen, and raising his glass. "Let's drink to parent-free homes."

"To parent-free homes," the women repeated, and sipped from their glasses.

"We should do something to reclaim our house. What do you think?" Rohan looked from Sameen to Tara.

Rohan's arm felt like a log on Sameen's shoulders.

Tara seemed to be studying the row of cookbooks on the shelf.

Still focused on figuring out what she was feeling, Sameen only half heard Rohan's question. "Hmm?"

"I know." Rohan clapped his hands, making Sameen jump. He swivelled to face her with a wide grin. "We should have a celebration. A biiig party!"

"A New Year's party?" ventured Tara.

"Yes." Rohan rubbed his hands together. "A theme party. Ooh, I know, Sameen and I saw this in a movie—let's have a celebrity fancy-dress party."

Rohan chattered on happily, clearly oblivious of the awkwardness in the room. Sameen sneaked a glance at Tara, who was giving her wine undue attention. She couldn't understand it. Why had things suddenly become uncomfortable with Tara? Was it because she'd walked in when she and Rohan were kissing? But this wasn't the first time they'd kissed in front of friends. Sameen had never felt so self-conscious about it earlier. So what was different this time?

What is happening to me?

Chapter 19

"WHAT'S THAT?" SAMEEN POINTED TO a giant pair of red lips on a stick.

"What?" asked Barkha with an innocent air. She was wearing a stunning silver off-the-shoulder gown, intricately embroidered all over, with a lacy band joining the bodice and the skirt, which showed off her midriff. Her hair had been carefully sculpted to fall over one bare shoulder. Her shoulders and neck were also speckled with glitter. She looked lovely and seemed completely oblivious to the cold—but that didn't explain her peculiar prop.

"Oh these? They are my lips," she said.

"Pardon?"

"I'm Priyanka Chopra," Barkha replied with a grin. She gave the lips a waggle. "Get it?"

Sameen laughed, shaking her head. "Very clever." She led Barkha away from the landing, towards the front door of her flat. "Hi," she said to Kunal, who was trailing Barkha.

He gave her a sheepish grin. He had on a (definitely designer) suit, a navy-blue silk tie, and white shirt. He'd done something odd to his hair.

"And you are?" Sameen asked.

He pointed to his head. "Don't recognize the bird's nest?"

"Right, hello, Mr Trump."

Kunal narrowed his eyes and took in Sameen's outfit. "And who are you supposed to be?"

Sameen had dyed her hair deep red and let it fall around her face in her natural frizzy curls. She had on a black dress, black stockings, knee-length leather boots, and a chunky black-and-blue-beaded necklace. Rectangular black-framed glasses completed her look.

Milind came up the stairs and grinned at Sameen. "Is that what she looks like, then, this Mona Eltahawy?"

"Who?" asked Kunal.

"A famous African journalist and author that Sameen has a crush on," Milind told him.

"Hey!" Sameen shook a finger in warning at Milind. "Behave. She is my new favourite author. And who are you, Random Bow-Tie Man?"

Milind patted his bow tie and straightened his jacket. "I like my martinis shaken, not stirred."

Sameen put her hands on her hips. "I said the theme was *celebrities.*"

"He *is* a celebrity," insisted Milind.

"There's a, um, Harry Potter coming up the stairs," Kunal pointed out diffidently.

"That's Ashish, my partner."

"Don't you two make the perfect couple," Sameen said. "Kunal, this is my misguided friend, Milind. Milind, Kunal—husband of Priyanka Chopra over there by the drinks table."

"Hi, Kunal." Milind shook his hand. "Come, let's get this party started."

Kunal followed him and Ashish inside, looking somewhat wary. Sameen didn't blame him. This was so different from the kind of parties he threw. Nearly thirty people must have been squeezed into the living room of the flat. Rohan and Sameen had moved the furniture against the wall, and some tables had been set up outside on the balcony for the drinks. Sameen wondered why Tara wasn't here yet. She couldn't wait to see which celebrity she'd chosen. Sameen hadn't seen her since the day Tara had walked in on Rohan and Sameen kissing. They had had different schedules at work and hadn't managed to catch each other since, though they had talked briefly on the phone a couple of times.

"Sameen, where are the rest of the glasses?" someone called out.

"I think they're in the kitchen," Sameen said. "Hang on, I'll get them."

She squeezed past the gaggle of guests and went into the kitchen, but Rohan was already taking care of the glasses.

"Everything under control?" she asked.

"Yup."

Sameen slipped into the bedroom to run a brush through her hair. When she came back out to her party, Milind pounced on her.

"There you are. Come see if you can guess who Tara is."

Sameen caught sight of Tara in that instant, talking to Barkha on the balcony. And that one glimpse was enough to take her breath away.

Tara had on a royal blue kanjeevaram silk sari with a double weave that gave it a maroon shimmer when she moved. It was dotted with tiny floral motifs and had a dark maroon-and-gold border. The blouse was a dull gold, and backless, the golden cord that tied at the back standing out against her skin. She wore a large blue bindi, and her hair fell in loose waves around her face.

As if by a secret signal, Tara turned around and looked straight at Sameen. For a couple of seconds, the air stilled around them. Then Tara smiled.

Sameen swallowed and forced herself to smile back. She went closer.

"Hey," she said, her mouth dry.

"Hey yourself," Tara replied.

"You came as Loveleen Bing?"

"I thought you'd find it funny."

"You look…breathtaking."

"She does, doesn't she?" Barkha put in.

Sameen jumped. She'd forgotten the others were there. She looked at Milind, who raised his eyebrows at her.

Tara put a hand on Sameen's shoulder. "Please get me a drink. I can't move much in these heels."

"Sure." Tara's hand was burning right through her dress but Sameen didn't want to move.

"I'll get it," Milind said. "Wine?"

"Red," Tara clarified.

"I'll come with you. I need a refill." Barkha gave Tara a lingering look as she followed Milind.

"So," Tara turned to Sameen, "you, um, look really…great." She didn't meet Sameen's eyes.

"Thanks." Sameen's face was warm and she felt stiflingly hot.

"I'm guessing you're Mona Eltahawy, the author you couldn't stop talking about."

"Yes." Sameen gave a laugh. It came out forced.

There was an awkward pause. The music became louder, and Sameen started as a pair of hands went around her waist.

"Dance?" Rohan said in her ear.

Sameen felt a stab of annoyance. But she smiled, took his hand, and allowed him to twirl her around and lead her to the dance area. The urge to turn back to Tara was almost overwhelming. She could imagine Tara's eyes on her, and the thought made her stomach clench with an unexplained yearning.

As Tara watched them go, a pinprick of jealousy nudged her, something she knew she had no right feeling. But what did she have to be upset about? They were a couple and she *had* to be okay with it. She had a wonderful friendship with Sameen. And that was as far as things between them could ever go.

"Red wine for you, Ms Bing." Milind's voice startled her.

She tore her eyes away from Sameen and took her drink. "Thanks." Her throat was dry. She gulped down a generous amount.

"Whoa, steady there, sister," Milind said. "You have those high heels to think of."

"What? Oh, right." She gave herself a shake and shifted a bit so Sameen and Rohan were no longer in her vision. "Is Ashish here? I haven't said hi."

"Come, then." Milind took her arm and led her back into the house.

Tara had no idea how time flew that evening. There was a pleasant buzz in her head from the wine as she stood against the railing outside, letting the cold breeze ruffle her hair. Barkha said something, and Tara laughed even though she barely heard her. Her gaze followed Sameen, who had come outside to help clear the table to serve dinner. She caught Tara's eye and smiled. Tara's heart fluttered.

Not again. This is supposed to be under control.

Tara was sure she had smiled, nodded, eaten, drunk, laughed, and maybe even danced a little that evening, but it had all been mechanical, on autopilot. Sameen was the only thing she could recall being aware of, like she was the north of the compass and Tara the needle.

"I should go help," she said half-heartedly.

Barkha stopped in the middle of whatever story she'd been telling. "You haven't heard a word, have you?"

"What?"

"Exactly. And no, don't you dare try to carry any food on those stilts while you're tipsy."

"I'm not tipsy."

"Then why does your tongue fall out each time you clap eyes on Sameen?"

"Barkha!"

Barkha pressed her lips together. "I tell it like I see it."

"Nobody wants to hear your rubbish."

Tara pushed herself off the railing and went inside, bristling at Barkha's words. Her feet were killing her. She figured Sameen wouldn't mind if she borrowed a pair of flats, so she went looking for the shoe cupboard.

Sameen and Rohan's bedroom a dumping ground for the guests' coats, shawls, and scarves. Deciding to take a breather, Tara sank down in the only available corner of the bed in relief. She closed her eyes and leaned sideways against the wall. Barkha's words came back to her. While Tara was used to her being about as blunt as a bludgeon, Barkha could be uncannily perceptive sometimes, especially about anything to do with Tara.

"Tara?"

Her eyes snapped open. Sameen was standing at the door.

"Everything all right?"

"Oh, er, yes," she said, slightly breathless. "I…just wanted a moment. And I borrowed a pair of shoes."

"Cool." Sameen shuffled from one foot to the other. "I should, um…" She gestured behind her.

"Yeah, yeah, of course."

"You should come get some food while there's still some," Sameen said as she turned away.

Tara reluctantly went back into the melee. Things were a lot quieter, as people were eating. The music had been turned down, and the walls were no longer vibrating. The neighbours must have heaved a sigh of relief.

Tara wasn't really hungry and pecked at her food. She and a few others helped clear up afterwards and, just as they were done, someone called out that it was five minutes to the new year.

An excited shout came from the balcony. "Fireworks!"

"But it's not midnight yet," Tara told someone dressed as Elvis.

"Someone's watch must be fast," Elvis responded.

Most of the guests had surged outside to watch the fireworks, which, from the sound of it, seemed pretty major. Tara decided that fireworks could wait and it was her bladder that needed urgent attention.

When she came out of the bathroom, the house was empty. Everyone was outside and, from the sounds filtering through, the fireworks were being much appreciated. She headed towards the kitchen to get some water.

As she turned into the kitchen, a movement startled her. Sameen unfolded herself from one of the cupboards under the counter.

"Oh, you gave me a fright," Sameen said. "Aren't you watching the fireworks?"

"I just came to get some water," Tara said.

"Let me get that for you." Sameen reached for the disposable glasses on the counter.

"No, it's okay," began Tara as she reached for them too. Their hands touched and a jolt of electricity ran through Tara.

Sameen's fingers moved along the back of Tara's hand and curled around her palm. Tara was frozen to the spot. They were so close, she could feel the heat radiating off Sameen. She could see her chest rise and fall, feel her breath on her face. She knew she should pull away *right now*, but her body refused to move. An unknown force held her in place, transfixed by the hand that curved around hers. Blood pounded in her ears. The shouts of "Happy New Year" seemed to come from another world.

"Happy New Year," whispered Tara. She raised her eyes to Sameen's. They were brighter, shinier than she recalled. Sameen held her gaze for a few moments, then her eyes dropped to Tara's mouth, and she leaned forward and pressed her lips to Tara's.

The world stopped. Tara felt like the ground beneath her feet had melted away and she was suspended in midair. When she closed her eyes, everything ceased to exist—the solidness of the floor under her, the walls of the kitchen, the sound of fireworks, and the people cheering outside. The only thing that remained was Sameen, and Sameen's soft, warm hands cupping her face and drawing her close.

Instinctively, Tara slipped her arms around Sameen's waist, drawing her even tighter to herself. Her familiar perfume filled Tara's senses. She groaned softy as she felt her body dissolve into Sameen's. An eager urgent need possessed her and aroused in her an awareness she hadn't thought she was capable of. Her heart felt like it would burst out of her chest as their bodies pressed close together, their tongues exploring each other with urgency. If this was a dream, Tara never wanted to wake up. But she knew it was no dream; it was a terrifying and exhilarating reality.

The arms that wrapped around Sameen's waist, feeling the warmth and the softness of her skin, seemed to belong to someone else. And yet, the way her heart filled with an inexplicable comfort which expanded to fill her entire body felt like a homecoming. Despite her senses screaming to stop, there was the other part of her that exulted in finally being able to do what she had been yearning to for a long time.

Something within Tara burnt as bright as the fireworks that were going off against the darkened night sky outside. She felt alive in a way that redefined the word. At every point her body touched Sameen's, it was as though her nerve-endings had been infused with an electricity that lit her up, inside and outside. All her bottled-up feelings for Sameen, the ones she had kept such a tight cap on, spilled out, threatening to sweep her away in a tidal wave of joy and thrill and a feeling of completeness. But all of it tinged by just a soupçon of sadness. Because even then, in that moment when all of Tara's defences lay breached, she knew deep down that this was not to be. And yet, if she couldn't have this, if she *didn't* have this, she had nothing, wanted nothing.

"Sameen, where's my Happy New Year kiss?"

Rohan's voice hit her like a splash of cold water. They sprang apart, and before anyone could move, Rohan bounded into the kitchen, his face red.

Tara didn't wait. She turned and walked away, faster and faster, till she was running down the stairs as quickly as her sari would allow.

Chapter 20

THE PINK-ORANGE STREAKS OF DAWN had started to paint the sky outside when Sameen realized she'd lain in bed for the past few hours. She couldn't even remember if she'd tossed and turned, or just remained motionless, staring at darkness, as sleep had remained elusive. She turned on her side, towards the window, and closed her eyes, desperate for some respite from the scene in the kitchen with Tara that played in her head for the millionth time. But every time she tried to close her eyes, she could see it even more clearly.

What had happened? And how? She had never been attracted to a woman. She'd had many boyfriends. Didn't that prove she was straight?

Was it because Tara was gay and had given out some sort of vibe that she'd subconsciously picked up on? But that didn't make sense either. They had an easy, comfortable friendship, and Tara had never expressed any interest in her as far as Sameen could recall. In fact, Tara had insisted she hadn't expressed an interest in anybody in ages. So what had happened at the party?

Where had all this come from? What was happening to her? Was she a lesbian now, or bisexual, or something else?

Sameen sat up and swung her feet to the floor. The chilled tiles under her jolted her to reality. It was bright outside now—which meant she had to have drifted off to sleep for a bit. But she felt far from rested. Her head was heavy, and a dull ache nestled between her shoulders. Even keeping her eyes open was more effort than she thought she could manage.

But she couldn't bear to think about *it* anymore. She rose and picked her way through the leftover mess from the party to get to the kitchen, which was an even greater mess. Her gaze lingered on the counter, where everything had happened.

She only realized she'd made herself a cup of tea when she held the steaming mug in her hands. She put it down, remembering she hadn't brushed her teeth, and immediately wondered if she was going crazy, thinking of brushing her teeth at a time like this.

Sameen went to the bathroom and then back into the bedroom. She pulled open her cupboard and absently picked out underwear, a pair of trousers, and a sweater to wear to work.

Rohan stirred when the cupboard shut with its customary click. "Uh…what are you doing?" he asked thickly.

"Getting dressed. I have to go to work."

"It's first January," Rohan said. "There's no work."

"Oh," Sameen said, staring at the sweater in her hand.

Rohan sat up suddenly. "Oh shit! I have a brunch meeting with Dayal! Aieee…" He held his head in his hands for a moment, then got out of bed and tottered to the bathroom.

When Rohan came out smelling of jasmine soap, Sameen was dressed for work.

"You're all jazzed up early in the morning," he said. "Where are you off to?"

"Office," said Sameen absently, leaning forward into the mirror to apply eyeliner.

"Sameen?"

The tone of his voice made her turn to him.

"We just had this conversation. It's a holiday."

Sameen looked down at herself. She didn't recall getting dressed. "Oh."

"Are you okay?"

"I-I'm really tired."

"Yeah, you look a bit peaky. Get back into bed."

"I should clean the house…"

"It can wait. We'll do it together when I come back."

Sameen changed back into pyjamas, heated her now-cold tea in the microwave, and went to see if the newspaper had arrived.

When Rohan came back late in the afternoon, she was still sitting on the sofa, and the newspaper was still lying rolled up on the balcony.

"Are you okay?" He looked worried and a little puzzled.

She was puzzled too. Where had the day gone? Rohan was looking around at the mess, just as it was from the party last night.

"Should we go to the doctor?"

Sameen shook her head. "I'm fine."

"You don't seem fine." He dropped his bag to the floor. "Have you eaten anything?"

But Sameen couldn't remember.

Tara sank into her chair with relief. Something about her poky little cubicle made her feel at home, even with its scuffed bulletin board and the slightly creaky wheel on her chair. The tippity-tappity of the keyboard and the intermittent hum of conversation from a couple of her colleagues covering a cricket Test match being played in New Zealand were the first things this morning that had made her feel normal.

She didn't have to come in today, but the other option was to go to her uncle's house for lunch, where the conversation would invariably drift towards her mother's recently abandoned husband-hunting project. And Tara *really* wasn't in the mood to deal with that.

She checked her official mail (only spam and press releases), then checked to see if there was anything she could update on the website (there wasn't). On a whim, she decided to check her personal mail, which turned out to be a bad idea. The top few mails in her inbox were old ones from Sameen.

Tara closed her eyes and rested the base of her palms against them.

Sameen.

This was such a disaster. She had been so *sure* she had her feelings under control. She had *promised* herself she would stay in control. What had she done wrong? How could she have let her guard slip?

Her throat hurt from trying not to cry. *What am I going to do?*

"Happy New Year," said a cheery voice. "Hangover?"

Tara jerked up to see her boss, Kabir, pass by with a wave, looking fresh as a daisy, as if he'd gone to bed by nine last night.

"Happy New Year to you too," she managed. She stared at the office door that swung shut after him.

A moment or two later, Tara went up and knocked, then edged the door open.

"Yes, Tara?" Kabir continued to frown at his monitor without looking up.

"I need to talk to you." She stepped inside.

Tara left his office fifteen minutes later, feeling a little shaky but definitely lighter. Barkha would probably have things to say, but she could deal with her later. Right now, she needed to keep her sanity intact.

Twenty-four hours later, Tara stood between an open suitcase and piles of clothes on the bed, mechanically transferring the piles from one side to the other. Her phone rang. She glanced at it—it was Barkha. Again.

Tara sighed and reached for it. She couldn't ignore her forever.

"Hi, Barkha. What's up?"

"What's up?" Barkha demanded. "You are asking *me* what's up? Why aren't you in office?"

"I have things to do."

"Yeah, I'll bet. What's this nonsense I hear about you switching assignments with Mike?"

Tara shifted her phone from one ear to the other. "Yes, I thought it'd be a change covering football—"

"What the hell are you talking about? Just last week you were going on about the Australian Open or T20 cricket or whatever. Now you're going off to an obscure village in West Bengal to cover some football tournament? When did this happen?"

Tara rubbed her forehead. So much was wrong with what Barkha had said that she didn't know where to start. "It's not an obscure village, it's Siliguri, and it's not just some football tournament, it's the—"

"Oh whatever. *Why?*"

"I just thought it would be a good change for me."

"Why do you need a change?"

"Just," Tara said.

"Tara, what the hell is going on with you? Something happened at the party, didn't it? You disappeared from there, and since then you've been incommunicado."

"Nothing happened."

"Really?"

Tara hesitated. "Really."

There was a silence. Then Barkha said in a flat voice, "Fine, then, if you don't want to tell me, I can't force it out of you."

The connection went dead.

Tara felt very alone.

Chapter 21

THE LETTERS SWIRLED BEFORE SAMEEN'S eyes, making no sense whatsoever. She exhaled loudly and slammed her pencil down on the proofs she had been marking. Sameen had been reading the same paragraph since she'd sat down at her desk, but still had no idea what it said.

She ran her fingers through her hair and groaned softly. This wasn't working. She opened her drawer and stuffed the proofs inside. Picking up her bag, she called to her assistant that she was leaving, and walked out of the office.

The sharp, cold air hit her face as she exited the building. She exhaled loudly, making a little white puff. She walked without really thinking where she was going. Her high-heeled boots were not conducive to walking, but she barely noticed the discomfort. She went on, one foot doggedly in front of the other.

When she finally stopped, she looked around in astonishment. Had she walked all the way to Green Park? She didn't even remember crossing the busy road at Yusuf Sarai. What must have been a half-hour walk seemed to have whizzed by.

Milind's place was just around the corner. It was as though a subconscious impulse had directed her to seek out what she needed. Sameen fished out her phone and dialled Milind's number. He picked up almost immediately.

"Hey, what's up?"

"Hi. I'm outside your house. Can you come out for a bit?"

He didn't ask any questions. "Sure. Be there in two."

It took him more than two minutes, but when he appeared, wrapped in a coat and woollen scarf, he had two cups of coffee with him. He offered one to Sameen, and without a word, he led her to the park, where they sat on a bench.

"What's wrong?" Milind asked.

"I kissed Tara," Sameen said without preamble.

"What?"

"You heard me."

Sameen closed her eyes. Her head was pounding. She thought saying what had happened would make her feel lighter, but it didn't. It only felt more messed up.

"What do you mean kissed? Was it a *kiss* kiss or a…"

"Stop being flippant. I'm trying to tell you something serious."

"No…I…sorry. What happened? Tell me from the beginning."

"We kissed, that's what happened."

"When?"

"At the party."

Milind felt for his coffee and accidentally knocked it over. Not bothering to pick it up, he turned back towards Sameen.

"Are you all right?"

"I don't know." Sameen dropped her head in her hands and squeezed her eyes shut to stop the tears from leaking.

"Do you want to tell me how it happened?"

"I don't understand it myself. It took me completely by surprise." She rubbed her face and looked up at the sky. "I don't know what to do."

Milind crossed his arms across his chest and stared down at the grass. He didn't speak for a few seconds. "Do you...are you... Do you think you're attracted to her?"

"I can't understand it. I love hanging out with her. She's been such a good friend. We have so much fun together. I feel like she gets me. But...I don't think I've ever thought of her as anything other than a friend." She swallowed. "That evening, I don't know what it was. The party, New Year's Eve, we'd both had a few drinks... I felt like...it felt different, Milind. I don't know. I know I keep saying that."

"Is that your way of saying yes, then?" he asked quietly.

Sameen looked at him directly for the first time. "What if I am? How will I know?"

Milind laughed. "Seriously?" He shook his head. "So, this kiss, it just happened?"

Sameen nodded.

"Who initiated it?"

"It's hard to say. I think we both went for it at the same time."

"Wow." Milind exhaled. "So she kissed you back?"

"Yep."

"And?"

"What do you mean 'and'?"

"I mean, did you like it?"

"I don't know."

Milind's eyebrows went skywards.

Sameen sighed. "Okay, yes. More than a little bit." Even now the memory of the kiss sent a thrill running down her spine.

"Well, there you have it. You were either too drunk to know what you were doing or you…"

"I wasn't drunk." *At all.*

Milind nodded slowly, his eyes on her. "So have the two of you talked about what happened?"

"No," Sameen said. "Tara's not been in touch. I haven't called her either."

"Are you going to? Don't say 'I don't know'."

Sameen shrugged. "What shall I say to her?"

"Well, for one, your friendship might be a bit dicey now, no?"

"I don't think I'm ready to talk to her yet."

"Okay, so the next question is, does Rohan know?"

Sameen dropped her head back into her hands. "No. Do I have to tell him?"

"You know the answer to that as well as I do."

Barkha:
Are you up? Call me.
-8:22 a.m.

Tara had barely had a moment to glance at her mobile. Even if she'd had the time, she likely wouldn't have responded to Barkha's demand to call. She was quite impressed Barkha had managed almost forty-eight hours of radio silence in the first place. Tara had been half afraid she'd be spending all her time warding off calls from her.

Tara had arrived in Kolkata the previous afternoon and then taken the night train to Siliguri. So far, she'd spent most of her time in press conferences and interviews. A number of international stars had been roped into playing for local teams in return for large sums of money, and for football-mad West Bengal, it was quite a treat. Tara liked football well enough, though cricket and tennis were her first loves. But then, it was a nice change for her—her work usually involved watching games on TV and writing about them—so she had been slightly taken aback at the hectic pace of the previous day and the packed tournament schedule. At first she'd had a serious case of repent-at-leisure-itis for the impassioned speech she'd given Kabir about her sudden interest in football, but she'd been a sports journalist for eight years, so getting into the swing of it hadn't been hard.

Most importantly, it kept her from coming apart about the Sameen issue. At the moment, she didn't care whether she was covering kabaddi or curling; all she wanted was to be away from all the familiar places that reminded her of Sameen.

Barkha:
> Missed call, 9:47 a.m.

Tara could barely stomach the thought of breakfast, but she forced down some toast. It sat like lead in her belly, but she took another bite because she had to eat. She sipped her lukewarm tea as she scrolled through her introductory story about the tournament. She still had to transcribe a couple of interviews, add some embellishments, and submit them by the end of the day. She hoped she'd get some work done before the day's itinerary made unreasonable demands on her.

Barkha:
What the hell, yaar. Are you ignoring me?
-10:01 a.m.

Gathering her laptop bag, Tara left her room and took the lift downstairs. Kabir always insisted that his employees travel and live well when they were touring, which Tara was thankful for. The irony did not escape her that Barkha had probably booked the hotel she was in. It was small, mostly catering to business guests, judging by all the formal clothes, serious expressions, and leather briefcases on display. As she walked towards the lobby, she saw one of the conference rooms being set up for a print-on-demand seminar. She wondered what print-on-demand was and why they would choose this town for a seminar about it.

Tara settled into a deep couch in the lobby to wait until it was time to leave for the stadium for an opening ceremony gala.

"Good morning, Tara." A slight, dapper figure stood next to her cough. It was Max Cheng, a journalist from Singapore, whom she'd met briefly a few years ago.

"Oh, hello, good morning." Tara smiled up at him, relieved to see a familiar face. "Are you going to the opening ceremony?"

"Yes, I am."

They decided to have a coffee while they waited, and later walked down to the stadium together. It was a pleasant, mild, winter's day, and soon Tara found herself watching schoolchildren perform various dances at the stadium and wondering what the hell this had to do with football.

Barkha:
Listen, are you bugged about waht I said at the party? I'm sorry, just me and my big muoth. Just call me pleeeease.
-12:15 p.m.

Barkha:
> Missed call, 1:12 p.m.

After the opening ceremony, one of the sponsors of the tournament held a lunch, to which all the participating teams, officials, and the media were invited. Max Cheng, it turned out, was rather well connected, and introduced Tara to some of the big names, who were kind enough to grant her interviews. So, instead of going to boring post-lunch media events, she spent an eventful afternoon talking to a forty-year-old Scottish footballer who had come out of retirement to play for a local team from Kolkata.

Barkha:
Oh Tara, what the hell is the mattter with you? Listen, don't pretnet that everythign is ok. I know something is wrong because this is classic you, giong into your shell when thigs go ape so just tell me taht your ok, okay!!!
-3:36 p.m.

Barkha was, for some reason, a stickler for grammar, and when her texts had typos, it was a foregone conclusion that her head was close to exploding. Tara bit down on her guilt. Barkha definitely didn't deserve this silent treatment, and she was only calling, emailing, and messaging so desperately because she was worried about Tara. But Tara wouldn't be able to hold it together if she started to think about the mess she'd left behind, even less so if she started to answer Barkha's questions, and delve into why she had kissed Sameen and what it meant.

So, instead, she returned to her hotel, ordered a cup of tea, and sat down to write a feature on the Scottish footballer. She'd found some interesting angles—Kabir would be delighted.

Barkha:
>Missed call, 5:44 p.m.

Barkha:
>Missed call, 6:09 p.m.

Barkha:
- Ok, fine, I give up. But this is not right, Tara.
-6:10 p.m.

That evening, a sports shoe company hosted a sponsor's dinner at the fanciest hotel in town. Tara steeled herself to attend. There was nothing better than dressing up, and wining and dining with strangers—okay, there *was* Max—to distract her from the mess that her life currently was. Indeed, it felt surreal, standing in the optimistically named Grand Ballroom of a hotel whose name she had already forgotten.

She felt like she had been playing a part. As though Sameen had been in a play Tara had acted in. Or perhaps that had been her real life and this was the play.

When she finally stumbled back to her room, it was past eleven p.m. and Tara's head felt like it was going to burst.

As she lay back on her bed with relief and closed her eyes, it crossed her mind that if all her days here were this hectic, she would barely have time to think about Sameen and the New Year's party.

But that didn't mean the heavy, black pit that was a mixture of dread, guilt, anger, grief, and pure helplessness lodged in her stomach was any lighter. That it didn't still feel as if it would tear her open.

Her hand hovered on the phone, charging on the bedside table. She wished she could talk to someone, just to hear a friendly voice. She considered calling her mother, but she would be in bed.

Tara's hand was still resting on the phone when it vibrated. She jumped. A split second later it rang. Tara sat up and stared at it.

The phone was face down, but she knew it would be Barkha. She might have said she'd given up, but when Barkha's antenna went up, it didn't come down until she'd unearthed whatever she was after. Tara had reached for the phone to decline the call, when she noticed the caller ID. Sameen's face was looking up at her.

Tara's heart jumped into her mouth, and the phone fell out of her hand on to the bed. Part of her wanted to answer so badly and to hear Sameen's voice that it hurt. Yet her body seemed to have turned to stone. Sweat broke out on her palms. Just the thought of talking to Sameen... Though it wasn't like she hadn't imagined an alternate reality where she could just talk to Sameen and everything would be okay.

But then, what would *okay* entail? Would it mean dialling back time and the kiss never happening? Or would it be... something else?

Heart thumping, Tara reached a shaky hand towards Sameen, who was still smiling at her, her eyes shining as they looked into Tara's, without a care in the world.

What would it take to just pick up the phone and tell Sameen the truth? That she'd fallen in love with her. That she wanted to give them a chance.

Did she dare?

Her thumb hovered over the green icon.

Her head was buzzing. She couldn't think anymore. She couldn't bear being alone any longer. Her thumb touched the screen just as the ringing stopped.

Chapter 22

THE SILENCE WAS DEVASTATING. ROHAN's hand remained frozen halfway to his mouth. The piece of chapati wrapped around a floret of cauliflower fell back on to his plate.

Finally, he broke the silence with a disbelieving "You did *what*?"

Sameen didn't reply. She just nodded.

"You mean, Tara kissed you?"

"Not exactly."

"*You* kissed her?"

Sameen squeezed her eyes shut. "It just happened."

"How can it just happen?" Rohan shoved his chair back, making the table screech back towards Sameen. He stood and rubbed his hands over his face. "Jesus!"

If Sameen had ever imagined telling Rohan would release the knot of dread in her stomach, she was sorely mistaken. It tore her apart all over again.

"Rohan, I'm—"

He stopped her with a wave of his hand. He was facing away from her, so she couldn't see his face. "How long has this been going on?" Rohan asked, his voice quiet.

"Nothing's going on."

"Don't lie to me, Sameen! You two spend so much time together. Is that it? Have you decided to become a lesbian?"

"Ro, nothing has been going on. It was just that day, just that one time."

"And? You didn't answer my question. Do you have feelings for her?"

Sameen swallowed. If only the answer were as easy as the question. "I-I feel so confused."

Rohan turned to her, his face a mask of shock, hurt, and anger. "You...you are...*confused*? *Confused?*"

He stared at her for a few moments, his face hardening. Then he turned and left the room.

"Rohan!" Sameen got up. "We have to talk about this. Please."

"I just need to clear my head," Rohan said, not looking back. The front door slammed with more than usual force.

And then it was back. That devastating silence.

Sameen stood still, not sure if she could move. She felt as if something had been scooped out from inside her. She wasn't sure how long she just stood there, numb. Then, her phone buzzed, jolting her back to reality. It was from Rohan, a message.

Staying with Sid tonight.
-9:33 p.m.

Sameen sank to the floor and let the silence take her.

Tara lay in bed and stared at the ceiling. She'd returned to her room a couple of hours ago. It was the first day of the tournament, and there had been three matches. She was knackered, but sleep eluded her. Like it had done ever since the New Year's party. She had relived her kiss with Sameen a million times, and each time felt more overwhelming than the last.

In the beginning, she had tried to stop herself from thinking about it, but the intensity of the memory was too strong. The intensity of what she felt for Sameen was too strong. She finally admitted that despite her better judgement and numerous efforts, she *had* fallen in love, once again. And this time, it was beyond her control. The realization of how much she cared for Sameen and that there was no future for them together made her sink into a deep, dark hole. She had never felt so lonely in her life.

A sudden knock on the door shook her out of her misery. It was probably room service with her dinner. Though she didn't have much of an appetite these days, the rational part of her knew she couldn't completely give up on eating. She got out of bed listlessly and pulled the door open.

"Barkha?" Tara whispered, unable to believe her own eyes.

"Hi," Barkha said, walking purposefully into the room and putting her travel bag on the floor.

Tara shut the door and faced her friend. Worry was etched all over Barkha's face. Something inside Tara broke.

As Barkha's arms went around her, she let herself go and allowed the grief she had kept dammed to engulf her. She clung to Barkha and sobbed like she'd never be able to stop.

Tara didn't know how long they stayed in that position. By the time she had composed herself somewhat, they were both seated on her bed. Barkha must have steered her there as she had held Tara, stroking her back and muttering unintelligible words of comfort in her ear. Tara took in huge gulps of air to calm herself.

"I'm so glad you came," she said, extricating herself from Barkha's arms. She plucked a few tissues from the box on the side table. Barkha got up and handed her a glass of water that was on the writing desk.

"Just tell me what's going on," she said, looking down at Tara. "Is it Sameen?"

Tara nodded, taking a sip. "We kissed."

"At the party?"

Tara nodded again.

"You really think running away is going to resolve anything?"

"I don't know."

"So then why did you do it?"

"I'm in love with her." Saying the words out loud was at the same time a great relief and a terrible burden. "I think I've been in love with her for a long time."

"Is that a reason to cut yourself off from everyone who cares about you?" Her tone was not harsh.

"I didn't know what else to do. I thought I had it under control. I thought I had put up these strong barriers around me that were impenetrable. But she broke through each one of them without my even realizing it. I got so scared. I had to get away from her."

"Oh Tara, you're so frustrating sometimes."

There was a knock, and Barkha rose and yanked the door open. This time it was room service with Tara's dinner.

"Could you get another one of these, please?" Barkha asked the waiter, pointing at Tara's order of chicken curry and rice.

He nodded and shut the door on his way out. Barkha turned back to Tara.

"You don't think talking to Sameen might have helped?"

"She's straight. She's with Rohan." *She's happy.*

"How straight can she be if she kissed you?"

"It was an accident."

"Doesn't she get to have an opinion, considering she is an equal participant in this situation?"

"What could I say to her? It's not like we can have a relationship or anything. I'm not going to pretend that we have a future."

"Listen, nobody's pretending anything. What you're doing is jumping to conclusions. You have this ridiculous excuse that you have used for years to justify not wanting to be in a relationship. The truth is you are scared of needing someone, of being vulnerable. It's been ten years since you broke up with Radhika because you claimed she wanted to be with a man. And you and I both know that's bullshit. The real reason you broke up with her was that you were scared. Just like you are now. You sabotaged your relationship then and you're doing exactly the same thing now. Have you learnt nothing in all these years?" Barkha ran her hands through her hair. "Listen, please, just talk to Sameen."

Tara shook her head. "It's no use. Nothing's going to come of it."

"This is ridiculous. You can't run from her forever."

"But I don't want a relationship!"

"Fine. Then at least try and save your friendship. Get some closure."

Tara sighed. "I'll think about it."

"That's all I ask. Now are you going to share your dinner with me or what? The service in this place is so crappy."

Chapter 23

Two weeks later, Tara came home from Kolkata and settled into her usual routine—from home to office and back. The only thing that was no longer part of this routine was Sameen. There was no sharing of taxis, no detour to tuck into delicious snacks, no hanging out endlessly in each other's homes, no watching and critiquing television shows to death, and definitely no sharing deep, dark secrets and being there for each other in the not-so-good moments.

Though the pain of missing Sameen had lost its sharp edge, it still remained as a permanent dull ache within Tara. She tried to ignore it by going about her daily life and distract herself by focusing on her work, but the more she tried, the less she was able to push it away. The grief seemed like it was there to stay.

Even though Tara had never been a very outgoing person nor had a roaring social life, she was starting to feel like the walls were closing in around her. It was a testament to how much Sameen had changed her. Six months ago, Tara would have been happy to potter around at home, cook something, watch TV, or do a jigsaw puzzle. Now the thought of going back to that life was stifling. It wasn't as though she'd suddenly become a party animal with Sameen, but some part of her had been slammed shut now that she was gone.

Even the jigsaw puzzles weren't that exciting anymore. Everything felt wrong. Lying in bed each night and scrolling through the photos of Sameen on her phone—photos she couldn't bear to delete despite her better judgement telling her that she needed a clean break—she knew she was turning into a cliché.

At least on workdays she had an escape, but when her off days came around, it was all she could do to get out of bed. Despite her natural restlessness, burrowing under the quilt felt like a refuge. The thought of facing yet another day without Sameen was too much to bear.

Barkha had started checking up on her at home, so when her phone rang, Tara snaked an arm out of her quilt and reached for it without checking the caller ID.

"Hey, wanna watch the latest Shah Rukh Khan movie with me?" Barkha asked, sounding criminally chirpy. "What's it called? I can never remember their names these days."

Tara had to smile. Barkha was so transparent sometimes. "If you can't even remember the name of the movie, why do you want to watch it?"

"Because Kunal has taken the kids to play minigolf."

"And you would rather die than spend your day pushing tiny white balls into holes with the apples of your eye?"

"Exactly. So are you coming with me?"

"Nah. I don't feel like it," Tara said, even though a part of her wished she could muster up enough energy to get out of bed.

"You wouldn't be avoiding me, would you?"

"Of course not. Why would you think that?"

But she knew exactly why Barkha would think that—because it was sort of true. She hadn't talked to Sameen despite promising Barkha that she would think about it. And she knew she wasn't going to do so anytime soon. Even though Barkha hadn't brought it up again, Tara could see the question in her eyes each time they met. Or maybe it was just her imagination. It was unlike Barkha to not say what she was thinking, and sooner rather than later, Tara would have to answer her persistent demand for an explanation.

Barkha made a noise that was a cross between disbelief and dismissal.

"I just feel like hanging out at home." Tara knew the excuse sounded as lame as it actually was.

"Isn't Chhaya there, inviting prospective grooms over to meet with you?"

"Fortunately, she's moved on to other things. She's cleared the study; there are no photographs or files in there anymore. The other day I was on the computer and failed to find any trace of her stupid research. I'm so glad this phase of her life is over."

"Has she found something else yet?"

"Who knows? She's been collecting travel magazines, but it's early days yet. You know how it is. There is a short lull before she goes full speed ahead."

"Yeah. It's like she's recharging her batteries before diving into something new."

Tara shuddered at the thought of whatever new project her mother would pick next. She ended the call with Barkha, and forced herself out of bed.

Her mother was sitting on the living room sofa reading a book on hill-station getaways when Tara came in with a bowl of cornflakes and settled down next to her. Chhaya took off her reading glasses and ruffled Tara's hair.

"Hey, sleepyhead. Catching up on your sleep lately?"

Tara shrugged.

"Sweetie, are you feeling okay? You seem a little down these days."

"I'm fine, Mama."

"I worry about you, you know."

"Don't. I'm fine."

Her mother sighed. "I know you're okay, but…I don't want you to be all alone. Who will look after you when I'm gone?"

"Mama, what's wrong with you? Why are you saying things like that?"

"You know, meeting your father, being with him, and then losing him made me realize one should never take love for granted. When you find it, you should respect it and nurture it. You must hold on to it with all your might because you never know when it will disappear."

The cornflakes turned to ash in Tara's mouth. She took a deep breath, put the bowl on the table, and gently clasped her mother's hands. "Mama, I know you want to see me get married, and I don't want to hurt you or be difficult, but it's not going to happen."

"I know." Chhaya sighed.

Tara's eyes widened. That was another loaded statement. Her mother returned her gaze, and Tara felt acceptance and understanding wash over her like a warm bath in winter. She understood then how much she needed her mother's support, and how easily she could have it whenever she needed it.

They sat in silence for a minute before her mother asked, "Why doesn't Sameen come around anymore?"

"What?" Tara blinked at her.

"Did you two have a fight?"

"It's complicated." Tara's voice caught in her throat.

"She's a good person, and good people are hard to come by. You must ask her to come over soon."

Not trusting herself to respond, Tara nodded. There were no words to explain to her mother what she was going through. She got up and stumbled into her room, no longer able to hold back her tears.

There was something magical about coming home to Bangalore, something almost surreal. Like entering a parallel existence where the complications of real life melted away into oblivion. Well, perhaps oblivion would have been stretching it somewhat, Sameen thought as she lay curled up in bed. It was more like her problems, her questions and dilemmas, the decisions she needed to make, and the things she had to sort out were all locked away in a box far, far away, and didn't need her attention as urgently as they had seemed to back in Delhi just last evening.

The familiar pale pink-and-yellow-printed curtains rippled by the window. Through the crack where the curtains didn't quite meet, Sameen could see a bright sunlit day outside. If she were to hazard a guess, she would say it was well past nine o'clock. That was another thing about being here—it was so easy to fall back into this whole cycle of waking up deliciously late.

Her stomach growled, reminding her that she hadn't had any dinner last night, what with the flight being so late. Masala dosas were probably waiting for her, with a steaming tumbler of homemade filter coffee, the welcome-home breakfast her mother invariably arranged whenever she returned to Bangalore. Yet her courage failed her at the thought of getting up and making her way downstairs and along the corridor to the big airy kitchen, where the ancient Revathi-akka, the cook, would take one look at her and set the griddle to heat to make fresh dosas.

Sameen turned on to her other side and stared at the wall. Despite having slept through what had been left of the night after she'd arrived, she felt like the energy had been drained out of her. She closed her eyes, the rhythmic squeaks of the fan swaying above her, lulling her back into a state of drowsiness.

Her phone pinged and she jumped. She reached for it automatically, for one insane second her heart leaping at the thought it might be Tara. A pang of guilt immediately ripped through her for not assuming it might be Rohan. But it was neither—just Vodafone welcoming her to Bangalore and telling her that she could have free 4G data if she clicked on the link.

She pulled herself up, her heart as heavy as the millstone Revathi-akka had used to grind rice when Sameen had been a girl. Her head spun with the sudden movement and she had to wait a moment before she could think of standing. The weight of all that had happened in the past few days came tumbling back to settle on her shoulders. The wall she had built to keep it all at bay crumbled in an instant, laying her pain bare.

"I can't do this," Sameen whispered, her voice breaking. Rohan's face rose unbidden in her mind again, the shock and hurt written all over it when she had told him about Tara. Whoever said the truth sets you free clearly didn't know what they were talking about. Look where the truth had brought her.

I am a bad person, Sameen told herself. *I promised Rohan forever, and then I turned away.*

Yet the thought didn't wreck her like she had imagined it would. She hated herself for that. And for feeling relieved that he had seemed to understand when she had said she needed time and space. He had reappeared the morning after her confession, his eyes red and downcast, and they had spent that entire week talking about nothing but this, rehashing Sameen's feelings, their relationship, the future.

She could see him standing at the door with his bags at the end of that week, this time saying he was going to step away until she figured out what she wanted. He had looked calm and collected from the outside, yet Sameen could see he was coming undone inside.

Though what was it exactly that she needed time and space to decide? On the one hand was the stable relationship with a person she had known for years, who she had been pretty sure was the one. And on the other hand was Tara.

How could she have feelings for Tara while she still loved Rohan? How could she hate herself for hurting him while her heart still yearned for Tara? How could two such conflicting truths exist?

How messed up am I?

She rubbed at her face as a noise at her door made her look up. It was her mother. "Oh good, you're up. Come on downstairs. Everyone wants to meet you."

"Already?"

But of course. There was a wedding in the family and that was always an excuse for added bonhomie.

She dragged herself to the bathroom to freshen up and get into some respectable clothes. As she walked downstairs and approached the drawing room, high-pitched laughter cocooned her and the uneasy veil of surreality descended again.

A gaggle of aunts and girl cousins had taken over the space, spread out on the various sofas and the floor. Tea and snacks were being passed around.

"Sameeeen!" Her cousin Shazia, the one the excitement was in honour of, leapt up from the floor and engulfed her in a hug. "Finally!"

She was pulled down on to the floor, squeezing in between Shazia and an ample elderly relative who pulled Sameen's cheeks like she was five.

"Sameen, my child, how you have grown."

"Uff, Aunty, you saw me only last year," Sameen protested.

The aunt gave Sameen a friendly smack on the arm. "I remember you from when you used to run around in my garden."

Sameen rolled her eyes at Shazia, and they giggled.

"Aunty hasn't forgiven you for all those trampled flowerbeds," Shazia said.

"We were just saying," Shazia's mother, a tall, thin woman seated on the sofa opposite, called out, "that after Shazia it will be you, Sameen."

"Me what?" asked Sameen an instant before she realized what they were talking about. She stiffened. "Oh."

"She should have been first anyway," said Shazia, "as she's older."

The last thing Sameen wanted was for the conversation to veer towards Rohan and the possibility of a wedding.

"Yeah, by two months." She nudged her cousin and rooted about in her head with desperate urgency for a change of subject. "So, all set?"

Shazia opened her mouth to respond, but the portly aunt on Sameen's other side got in first.

"What is this I hear about some boy back in Delhi, Sameen? Have you set a date?"

"A date?"

"Of course. For the wedding. Are you planning to do it all in secret? Ha ha ha."

Sameen attempted a grin.

"Roshan, is it?" a much-older cousin asked.

"Rohan," Sameen said weakly. Her head pounded.

"Hai," another aunt lamented, slapping a hand to her chest, "Shazia marrying Baljeet, and now Sameen and this Rohan. What's wrong with these girls? Are there no more good Muslim boys anymore?"

There was a second of uncomfortable silence.

Then Shazia piped up. "No, Aunty, your generation gobbled them all up."

Laughter filled the room as Sameen dragged herself up, muttering something about going to get breakfast.

Chapter 24

A GLITTERING BEJEWELLED AUNT SIDLED up to Sameen at the buffet line and nudged her in the ribs. "So," she said, nodding over her shoulder, "is he the one? What a handsome chap."

Sameen's eyes flew wide open. She looked to where the aunt was gesturing, half afraid Rohan had indeed turned up. But all she saw was a group of obscure male relatives, plates in hand, laughing at something. Then she spotted Milind in their midst.

"No, no, of course not," Sameen said, annoyed. Why was it that the more distant the relationship was, the more these aunts felt they had a right to poke into your private affairs? "That's Milind. Don't you remember him?"

A many-ringed hand flew up to the aunt's mouth. "Milind? The same Milind you went to school with? Oh my, he's changed so much. He was so skinny and he cut off his curly hair. Is he married?"

Sameen gave a snort that she hurriedly turned into a cough. She wondered whether the truth would give the nosy aunt a heart attack. "No, but there's someone."

The aunt was now piling biryani on her plate, seeking out the choicest pieces of mutton without shame. "All the girls in the family are married now. It's just you left."

A knot formed in her stomach. The fragrant biryani suddenly made her nauseated.

"I'm not sure I'm ready," Sameen said truthfully. "Or that I will be anytime soon."

"Nonsense. You're almost thirty. What do you have to be ready for?"

Sameen slammed her plate down on the serving table between the mutton biryani and the malai koftas, and turned away, ignoring the indignant cries of the offended aunt. There might be words later about her rudeness, but she didn't care.

She cut through the tables set all over the lawns, weaving between groups of overdressed guests, and made for the hotel lobby. Apart from a lone woman at the reception desk and a couple of guests, it was empty. She sank down into a sofa and closed her eyes.

Sameen felt the cushion dipping as someone sat next to her. Opening her eyes, she found Milind crossing an elegant leg carefully over another and brushing out the creases in his sherwani. "I saw you running away," he said by way of greeting.

"Some old bat was trying to marry me off to you."

"Oh dear. Been that sort of night, has it?"

Sameen sighed. "And this is just the engagement party. How am I going to get through the rest of this?"

Milind took her hand. Then, noticing a couple of giggly teenage cousins of Sameen's watching them, he let it go hurriedly. "Look at it as a distraction?"

"I can't. It's…the more I try to push it away, the more it pushes back."

"Have you considered," Milind said carefully, "not pushing it away?"

She had. Of course she had. "I want to go home. Will you come with me?"

"Sure."

Sameen texted her mother saying she wasn't feeling well, and they took a taxi back. Milind was staying at her parents' place as well.

"You know," she said, breaking the long silence on the drive home, "I never asked Rohan what his parents thought of me."

"Why is that?"

"I don't know. Maybe because I didn't want to hear the answer. What it would mean if they said they liked me."

"Sameen, do you love Rohan?"

Yes, of course she loved him. But it wasn't so simple. She was lucky to have him. But being married to him? Panic welled within Sameen at the thought. Neither of them had been in a hurry to get married, but the thought had never scared her in the past. It had seemed inevitable even, and not such a bad thing at all. But something had changed in the past few months, and it made her question everything she had taken for granted. It wasn't just the kiss with Tara; it was something from before that. She didn't know what that thing was, but it had made her wonder whether there was something else, something more that life had to offer. A feeling of "Is this it?"

Despite the darkness, she knew that Milind was watching her. "Can you be in love with two people at the same time?" she asked.

Milind didn't move. It was as if he hadn't heard her. Then he turned away, looking out the window as the buildings rolled by. "That's what I was afraid of," he said, his voice soft.

"You knew?" Sameen asked incredulously.

"It wasn't rocket science. Seeing the two of you together, and especially on the night of the party. And then, this past month. I've never seen you so low, Sameen. And I know it's not because of Rohan."

"He's a good guy," Sameen said. "He said he'll wait for me till I figure it out."

"I know he is a great guy. But," Milind turned back to her, "you have to be honest with yourself."

"What's it like to be gay?" Sameen asked.

Milind's eyebrows rose. "What?"

"I said—"

"Yes, I heard what you said." He exhaled loudly. "It feels, I don't know, normal? If I were to guess, when it comes to falling for someone or being attracted to someone, I don't suppose it feels any different from being straight."

After they reached home, Sameen went off to change out of her finery while Milind made some hot chocolate. When she came back dressed in her pyjamas, he'd switched on the lights in the dining room. They sat at the corner of the six-seater dining table.

"Does it matter?" Milind asked.

"Does what matter?"

"What you call yourself. Gay, straight, bisexual, whatever."

"I don't know. Does it matter to you?"

"It's complicated. It matters when I'm angry that the world at large recognizes only one form of love. I'm sad that my parents won't talk to me. But when it really comes down to our everyday lives, Ashish's and mine, it doesn't. As long as we can make it work, I don't really care what I call myself."

Sameen knew what he meant. Things hadn't been easy for Milind ever since he'd decided he wasn't going to lie to his parents anymore, even if it strained their relationship. On the other hand, he'd been more or less "adopted" by Ashish's family even though Ashish wasn't out to them. Welcoming Milind into their fold hadn't stopped them from pestering Ashish to get married—they just hadn't made the connection between Ashish's refusal to consider marriage and Milind's presence.

It was ironic that the same space—the family—that could be so conservative could also be completely open to accepting one's friends without hesitation. They hadn't asked any questions or demanded any explanations—"any friend of our son's is like our son too" was good enough. Ashish didn't care what they thought because he didn't think he owed anyone an explanation. The only thing that mattered was that Milind was accepted as part of his family.

"Tara thinks same-sex relationships are not possible in this country."

"I wouldn't say that," Milind said. "Of course, it's not a bed of roses either. It's difficult everywhere in the world, more so in some places than others. But are you supposed to wait for things to get easier before living the life you want, or do you fight to make a better life for yourself? By 'fight' I don't necessarily mean making a grand statement—which is also important—but that you work within the system and you make whatever little space you can for yourself. That itself is an act of pushing the boundaries. Knowing that in doing so you are making way for a different future, not just for yourself but for other people too. Even enabling people like Amma and Appa to see that there are other ways to be happy."

"I never knew you felt this way. You've never said anything."

"You never asked. And anyway, I thought you'd laugh at me."

"I could never laugh at you about something like this." But the rest of it was true, she supposed. Strange how close she and Milind were, but she had never thought to ask him about such an important part of his life.

"Think about it," Milind said. "In some ways you and Rohan probably raise many more eyebrows than Ashish and I do. You are 'living in sin', whereas we are roommates for some people, good friends for some, and life partners for others."

Sameen gave a dry laugh. "That's true."

"Sameen, let's cut the crap, shall we? I've seen you swirl into a funk over the past weeks and I think it's time for some straight talk." Milind leaned forward, elbows on his knees, looking directly at her. "Stop thinking, stop trying to make sense of it. Just tell me what you feel."

Sameen stared back into his dark brown eyes. His gaze went straight into her, like he could see what was in her mind anyway.

"I fell in love with Tara," she said softly. "Long before the kiss. I just didn't know it. But I know she doesn't want me and I don't know how I can live with that." A tear rolled down her cheek.

Milind took her hand and pulled her into his arms. She held on to him with all her might, like she would sink without him. Her heart was weighed down with a grief she found too hard to bear, but her head felt light.

If this was the famed year-round good weather of Bangalore, then the people here had a very warped definition of what good was, Tara thought. It was warm enough that she'd had to shed the layers she'd set out from Delhi in. She was now just down to a shirt. It was a change from not being able to feel your nose, but she hadn't expected to be sweaty.

Even though she was feeling slightly let down by the weather, there was something else about Bangalore Tara loved. That would be the people, who did not wait to find out who you knew and who you were friends with before deciding to be nice to you. This was unlike Delhi, which was bursting at the seams with snobs, especially if you happened to move in certain circles.

This time, however, after weighing up all the pros and cons, Tara wished she was back in Delhi. She couldn't stop thinking that Bangalore was Sameen's hometown. That her parents lived in this city. Sameen had told Tara a little bit about her childhood, and the memory of those conversations had come flooding back as soon as she had stepped out of the plane the previous night. She wished the pain that usually accompanied thoughts of Sameen would spare her this time, but she'd had no such luck. It remained lodged in Tara's heart.

Since she had no choice but to get on with her day, Tara headed out of her room at the Garden Palace Hotel. She had an appointment with the former cricketer Rahul Dravid, who was going to meet her in the lobby in ten minutes and talk about the coaching school he was setting up. She was about to enter the lobby when she heard a familiar voice.

"That was the worst buffet menu I've ever seen. Whatever possessed the alumni committee to choose this place?"

Tara turned the corner and froze. Milind was standing in the corridor. With Sameen. She had her back to Tara, but Tara would know her anywhere.

Tara *had* to be dreaming. The last person she'd expected to run into, the one person she thought was safely back in Delhi, couldn't be standing in front of her on her first day in Bangalore. Could she? There were eight *million* people in this blasted city, for heaven's sake.

Or was Tara completely losing it?

"Tara?" Milind said.

Tara's heart thudded against her ribcage as Sameen turned.

"Hi," said Tara as Sameen's eyes widened.

"Hi," Sameen replied, looking bewildered.

If Tara had let them, her knees would have buckled. Remaining upright took all her willpower. She drank in Sameen with her eyes. She wanted to reach out to her, to touch her and hold her. She wanted everything to stop—time, the world, the universe—so that this moment, this impossibly painful and yet completely wondrous moment, would remain eternally frozen, like a fly trapped in amber, giving her a "forever" with Sameen.

"Tara, what a pleasant surprise!" Milind's voice was full of incredulity, shattering Tara's illusion and rudely dumping her back to reality. "What are you doing here in Bangalore?"

She forced herself to look away from Sameen and addressed Milind. "Work. We're doing a series on cricket coaching centres around the country..." She trailed off.

"That's nice," Milind replied politely.

An awkward pause followed as nobody looked at anyone else. Then Milind patted his jeans pocket.

"I...think I left my phone in the bathroom. Be right back."

He walked away. Tara was pretty sure she had seen the outline of a phone when he had felt his pocket. Her eyes hungrily took in every familiar line, every curve on Sameen's face.

"How are you?" Sameen asked, breaking the silence.

"Well," lied Tara. "And you?"

Sameen nodded. "Yeah." Tara saw her swallow. Sameen had lost weight. She couldn't exactly be described as slender, but she definitely looked diminished.

"Are you visiting your parents?"

"Yes. My cousin's wedding."

"Oh, right. Shazia?"

"Yes."

Tara nodded. "So…um…where's the wedding?"

"In court, on Monday."

"I see."

Tara struggled to find something else to say, but nothing came to mind.

"Uh…I think I'll go see if Milind's found his phone," said Sameen after a few seconds of strained silence. She stared at the floor between them. "It was nice to see you, Tara," she said softly and turned in the direction Milind had headed.

"Sameen, wait!" The words were out of Tara's mouth before she could stop herself.

Sameen turned back and looked at her with a questioning expression.

"Will you have coffee with me?"

Sameen frowned. "Why?"

"We…we should talk."

"I called you. Several times. But you didn't take my calls."

This time Tara could hear the controlled anger in Sameen's voice.

"Yes, I know. And I'm really sorry I didn't call you back," she said. "Will you please give me a chance to explain? Meet me for coffee. Please?"

Sameen regarded her intently. Tara waited with bated breath for her decision.

"All right. When and where?"

Tara exhaled. "How about tomorrow? Matteo on CMH Road. Do you know it?"

Sameen nodded. "What time?"

"Five?"

"Okay."

"Okay. Thanks."

Sameen nodded again. "I'd better be going now. Bye." She walked away.

"Bye," said Tara, but she couldn't be sure if Sameen had heard her.

Chapter 25

SAMEEN ENTERED MATTEO ON THE dot of five. She glanced around to see whether Tara had arrived, then headed towards the far end of the coffee shop to grab a table near the window when she didn't spot her. As she watched the cars whizzing by on the busy road outside, she wondered what she was doing here.

After the initial shock of having come face-to-face with Tara, the anger she had been holding at bay flared again. It smashed through whatever bottle it had been stoppered in and flowed into every cell in her body. Yet even then, all it had taken was for Tara to look at her with her big, wide eyes, and here she was.

How was it possible that the person who could make her so furious was also the person she couldn't imagine her life without?

She looked at the door as Tara walked in, and her heart skipped a beat. Strange how she'd never recognized her feelings for what they were before.

"Hi." Tara slipped into the seat across from her. "Have you been waiting long?"

Sameen shook her head. "I only arrived a couple of minutes before you."

A server showed up to take their orders.

"Just a cappuccino for me, please," Tara said, then looked questioningly at Sameen.

"Make that two."

They sat in silence for a few seconds before Tara said, "Thanks for coming. I wasn't sure if you'd be here."

Sameen shrugged.

Tara picked up the glass of water that the server had just placed in front of her, took a sip, and cleared her throat. "I'm not sure where to begin."

"How about you start with telling me what I'm doing here."

Tara's finger made little circles on the table. "I thought we could talk about what...happened."

"You mean you want to talk about the kiss?"

Tara shifted in her chair and clasped her hands together. "Um...uh...yes."

"Don't you think it's a bit late for that?"

"Sameen..."

"Why now? Where were you when I made so many attempts to get in touch, tried to call you so many times? Why didn't you pick up the phone? Did you ever think about calling me? My whole world came apart after that kiss. Where were you then, when I needed my best friend to help me make sense of what had happened? Tell me what's changed now?"

Sameen looked around, aware that she needed to keep her voice low. But the object of her anger was finally in front of her and she couldn't stop herself from lashing out.

Tara seemed to be unable to meet her eyes. "I don't have the words to tell you how sorry I am. Things happened between us that I couldn't deal with. They scared me, and the only thing I could think to do was take myself away from the situation."

"So why are you here now?"

"Because I miss you. I miss our friendship. I know my behaviour caused you a lot of distress and severely damaged our friendship, but I want to try and repair it if you'll let me."

"Friendship? You don't know the meaning of the word. Friends don't get scared and run away when the going gets tough. They stick around and fight. They fight to keep the friendship alive. But you abandoned what we'd worked so hard to build. You abandoned *me*. Do you have any idea what you've done?"

"I do. I know. And that's why I'm here. I made a colossal mistake. I wish I could take it back. But I can't. All I can do is hope you will accept my apology."

"Cappuccino, ma'am," the server interrupted. They sat in a tense silence while she placed their coffees before them.

Sameen gripped her coffee mug hard, unmindful of how hot it was. The server's arrival had halted the momentum of their conversation. Perhaps it was for the best.

"So that's what it was, then, a mistake?" she asked in a low voice.

"We had a wonderful friendship, and I wrecked it with that kiss. I'm so sorry, Sameen."

Sameen was shaking. *A mistake.* That's what Tara thought it had been. A mistake. The words pounded inside her head. They filled her up, pushing against her skin and bones, fighting to come out and shred her to pieces.

And then, she was seething all over again. None of Tara's explanations made any sense. But Sameen couldn't let Tara see how her words were ripping her apart. If she wanted to leave here with any semblance of dignity, she had to get a hold of herself.

She took a deep breath and nodded. "If it was such a mistake, why did you let it ruin our friendship? Why did you run away?"

"Because I fell in love with you," Tara said. It seemed like the words were being wrenched from her.

The pounding in her head was back, and this time it was for a different reason. Sameen was sure she'd heard wrong. *Fell in love?* Since the kiss, Sameen had hoped and dreamed about the moment when Tara would confess her love for her, but she had never in a million years thought it could become a reality in this manner. It seemed cruel. Like someone was playing a mean joke on her. And it still didn't make any sense. If Tara loved her, why had she disappeared from her life?

"I tried very hard to not love you" Tara's voice shook as she went on. "But I failed. Remember that time when I became incommunicado for a bit after your accident? That's when I started developing feelings for you. Then, when you came looking for me, I thought I could deal with my feelings by ignoring them. But our kiss happened and I knew that what I felt for you was beyond my control."

"So that's your thing, then?" said Sameen, her voice shaking too. "Running away? Instead of just telling me?"

"If I told you, it would've seemed like I was asking you to return my feelings, which I can assure you is not the case even now."

"Isn't that for me to decide, whether I return your feelings or not?"

"But it wouldn't be fair."

"Why wouldn't it be fair? After what happened at the party, you didn't even think to ask me what I thought?"

"I don't want anything from you except your friendship. I don't do relationships. You know that."

A lump had lodged itself in Sameen's throat like an unwanted guest. "Why are you telling me all this now?"

"Because I owe it to our friendship. I shouldn't have taken off like that. We should have talked about it, you're right, and worked things out together."

"Like I said before," Sameen said, looking out of the window, "it's a little late for that." She stared at the street again, wondering whether coming here had been a mistake.

"How's...er...Rohan?" Tara asked, breaking the tense silence that was starting to engulf them.

"I'm sure he's well, wherever he is."

"You broke up?" Tara's voice had an edge to it, making Sameen turn towards her. A frown of bewilderment was etched on her face.

"Not exactly. We're taking a break. Things had been getting a little difficult, but now they seem to be becoming clearer. I think it's about time we talked."

"I'm glad. You two are good together."

"I don't know... Maybe this is as good as it gets."

"Maybe."

They looked down at their coffee cups.

"Sameen?"

"Hm?"

"Can I call you sometime? I know the cracks in our friendship will take time to heal, but could we try to start mending them as soon as possible?"

"I don't think that's a good idea."

"I see." Tara looked back down at her coffee.

"I'm not sure you do."

"What do you mean?"

"You might not want a relationship, but what I feel for you is too strong for me to be your friend. If I am around you, I will always want more. So it's best for both of us if we stayed away from each other."

Tara's eyebrows shot up. "Sameen…are you saying that you…you…"

"That I had feelings for you? That I fell in love with you too? Yes, Tara, I was stupid enough to do that."

"But…" Tara began.

"But what? Why I didn't tell you?" Sameen's laugh was sardonic. "*Really?* There are no buts anymore. We've both placed our cards on the table and made our moves. We have to respect the rules of the game."

A fist squeezed Sameen's heart as Tara nodded through the tears that filled her eyes.

Sameen looked away, picked up her bag, and stood. "Take care, Tara," she said and walked out of the cafe.

Only when the door shut behind her did Sameen let the tears come.

"She said she fell in love with me." Tara's voice sounded hollow even to her own ears. "She fell in love with me. She said that."

Even though she was saying the words, they felt unreal to her. Each time she said them out aloud, or even thought them, they seemed to disintegrate in the air around her, like they were mocking her.

Barkha exhaled noisily through her teeth. She crossed her legs up on her bed and settled in comfortably against a pile of cushions. "What are you going to do?"

Perched at the other end of Barkha's king-sized bed, Tara lay her forehead on the arm that she rested on her drawn-up knees. "I don't know," she mumbled.

"Do you still love her?"

"Of course I do."

"And she loves you. I don't see a problem here, Tara." Barkha's voice dripped with the sort of studied patience that only indicated she was feeling anything but.

"Don't you see?" Tara looked up. "It's all so messed up. She's going back to Rohan now."

Barkha held up a finger. "You said she's going to talk to Rohan. To be fair, you don't know what that means."

"What I do know is that she doesn't want to be with me." She let her head drop back on to her arm.

She expected Barkha to respond, to say something, even to mouth some platitude. But there was only silence. The seconds stretched to about a minute, then the bed moved as Barkha got up. She heard the shuffle of Barkha's slippers on the polished marble tiles. They went to the end of the room, then came back and stopped next to her. Tara raised her head.

Barkha's arms were crossed and she watched Tara with the sort of intense scrutiny one would give to an incomprehensible puzzle.

"What?" Tara asked.

"I don't know if I should say it."

"Say what?"

"Exactly. I don't know if I should say it."

"You're going to give me the hairdryer treatment, right?"

Barkha's brow furrowed. "What treatment?"

Tara shook her head. "I mean the way Alex Ferguson used to yell at his Manchester United team... Never mind. Just say it. You know you're going to. Eventually. And I probably need to hear it."

Barkha stared at her for another few moments. "This is the only chance you're going to get," she said, her voice quiet.

"Only chance for what?"

"To get Sameen back."

"I told you, she doesn't want to be with me."

"See, that's the problem with you. You sit around on your high horse and make assumptions. You never actually do anything about the important things. You never ever tried with Sameen. You never told her what you really felt, you were never honest with her. You just jumped into a box and slammed the lid shut, and pretended that if you didn't face what was going on, it would cease to exist."

"I—"

"You say you loved her," Barkha ploughed on, "that you still love her, but nothing you've done makes me believe that you actually do. You are in your thirties, but you're letting some idiotic teenage romance and heartbreak decide the course of your life. What happened with you and Radhika wasn't a template for all your future relationships, you know.

"Look around you, Tara. Life happens—it happens to all of us—and we move on, and we adapt and change, and we do what it takes to make things work. It's time you grew up and figured out some things about yourself and your life. It's time to be honest with yourself and about what makes you happy." Barkha's voice was still calm. She didn't seem angry or impatient as she usually was whenever she doled out life lessons to Tara. "Right now you are choosing misery."

Barkha's words hurt, but Tara was at a point where she had no defences against them. Her shoulders drooped.

"You're right," she said. "I've spent all this time thinking I had no choice. It's true that I don't know for certain if Sameen is getting back with Rohan, but then, what have I ever done to make her believe she might have a future with me? I never even had the courage to tell her that I loved her until it was too late. For all she knows, I've never been interested and that kiss was a mistake. I never made her believe that she could choose me. I couldn't even be a good friend to her."

"Exactly. Now that you seem to have finally stopped feeling sorry for yourself, what are you going to do?"

Tara sighed. "I think I need to be honest with myself and with Sameen, and find the courage to face whatever that brings. And if she then slams the door in my face, at least I'll know I tried"

"Now we're talking." Barkha yanked Tara off the bed. "What are you sitting around for?" She shoved her towards the door. "Go get your girl!"

Chapter 26

SAMEEN'S PHONE VIBRATED IN HER purse, but she didn't feel like answering it or even checking to see who was calling. Sitting on a bench outside the sub-registrar's office at the district court, waiting for Shazia and Baljeet to be called inside, Sameen couldn't help wondering if one day this was going to be her story too, marrying Rohan in an impersonal civil ceremony, where everyone was bored to death with all the waiting. The thought left her cold.

The bench creaked as her brother, Danish, sat next to her. "I never realized this would be so damn mind-numbing." He had his eyes firmly fixed on his phone as he scrolled and clicked his way steadily through his Facebook feed. "I'm never doing it."

"Well, good for you."

"Your phone is ringing," Danish pointed out. "Someone's calling you."

"Thanks, genius."

"You're welcome." he said with a sickening-sweet smile.

A hassled court official bustled out of a room with a file under her arm and called out, "Baljeet Singh Batra and Shazia Siddiqi."

A flurry of excitement ensued as Shazia and Baljeet's party of family and friends—a motley crew of about a dozen—rearranged themselves. The court official ushered the couple, along with their witnesses, into the office, all the while trying to explain to the rest of them that they would just have to wait outside.

Sameen extricated herself from the gaggle of relatives trying to argue their way inside and stepped out into the courtyard. It was a cool day—sunless thanks to the threatening rain. Her phone rang again and she fished it out.

Tara's name stared at her from the lock screen. Three missed calls.

Sameen's heart thudded. She stared at the screen till it gently faded to black once again.

For weeks, she had hungered for Tara to call or even message. She hadn't and, worse, all of Sameen's calls and messages to her had gone unanswered. She had yearned to hear Tara's voice, albeit as a poor substitute for seeing her in person. But after meeting her last weekend and clearing the air—although that was a completely unsuitable term for the heated and charged exchange they'd had at Matteo—Sameen was left feeling like she was drowning. The tangle of emotions roiled inside her, more turbulent and furious than before.

After all this time of shutting her out, after Sameen had finally had the opportunity to tell Tara how she felt and that she wanted nothing more to do with her—even though saying that had felt as if she were tearing herself in two—Tara thought *now* was a good time to call? It was like poking a red-hot stake into the open, festering wound that was Sameen's heart.

"She's bloody fucking unbelievable," Sameen said under her breath.

Yet all she wanted to do was call Tara back. A tiny part of her heart still filled with joy at the thought of hearing Tara's voice.

She pressed the power button again to light up the screen and stared at Tara's name. It would be so easy to just call her and say, "Forget what I said. I'll take anything, even friendship."

Her heart continued to race, and she had a sensation of being outside her own body, watching herself from a distance. She saw a youngish woman in her new blue salwar kameez, lost to the world, staring at her phone uncertainly, probably wondering whether to make a call. Around her, people milled, some hassled and worried; others drank tea from small earthen cups; some talked on the phone; lawyers, recognizable by their white bands, walked purposefully in and out of the building—

Someone bumped into Sameen's side, sending her stumbling into the wall and jerking her rudely back to reality.

"Ma'am, are you okay?"

An apologetic elderly man was handing her phone back to her. She must have dropped it. "I'm so sorry. I tripped and I couldn't stop myself and—"

"It's all right," Sameen said. "I'm fine."

"Are you sure?"

"Yes, I am." She forced a smile. "Are you okay?" The files the old man had been carrying had scattered to the ground, loose papers falling out. She helped him gather them back together.

With the files rescued and the man on his way, Sameen sat on the bench by the wall. She was much calmer thanks to the distraction, but she didn't trust herself. She fished out her phone and dialled Milind.

"Hi? All done?" His familiar voice took her stress level down another notch.

"Not yet. Shazia and Baljeet have just gone in. Listen, Milind, I'm freaking out a little bit."

"What happened?"

"Tara." Her palms were getting sweaty. "She called…three times."

For a few moments Milind didn't say anything. "Wow. Did you speak to her?"

"No. I-I… No, I didn't."

She could almost hear Milind thinking. "So," he said after another few seconds of silence, "did you want to?"

Sameen sighed. Now that he'd put his finger on the problem so accurately, it was difficult not to face facts.

"I don't know… I feel I can't deal with this now. Not after our talk, you know. What if she calls again?"

"Are you sure you don't want to speak to her?"

I do want to speak to her. More than anything else.

She might as well have said that out loud, because Milind, without waiting for a response, continued. "Okay, listen, don't stress about it now."

"What do I do if she calls again?"

Sameen wasn't unaware of how the tables had been turned. This time she was the one ignoring Tara's calls. *But this is different*, she tried to reason with herself. *I have told her not to contact me.*

"You can block her or switch off your phone or keep talking to me," Milind said. "Shall I come and get you?"

Somehow that mundane question made something snap back in place for Sameen. "No, of course not. I'll be fine. I just panicked for a moment."

"Sure?"

"Yeah. Thanks, Milind."

"Anytime."

Tara's chair creaked as she leaned back and stretched her arms over her head. She yawned and rubbed her eyes. Lack of sleep plus too many hours staring at the computer was not a good combination.

Her eyes strayed to her phone, lying face down next to her monitor. It was on silent mode, a new tactic these past few days to stop herself going crazy wondering if Sameen would call back or reply to her texts.

Not that this didn't drive her nuts in a completely different way—the anticipation and the endless waiting before she would let herself check her phone again. She glanced at the time on her desktop. Another fifteen minutes before she was "permitted" to check, but then, she'd finished her story and submitted it well before time, so she was allowed a pass.

She reached for the handset, turned it over. And her heart sank. Again.

Before she could think about it, she pulled up Sameen's contact information and dialled. It rang once, then a recorded voice told her the number was busy. She was pretty sure that meant Sameen had blocked her.

She lobbed the phone on to her desk and pushed her chair backwards to reach for the bottle of water behind her. Through the opening of her cubicle, she could see Barkha, Mike, and a couple of others out on the balcony, taking a smoke break. She wondered what comfort smokers found in their ciggies. Perhaps she needed a drag of whatever poison was in them to incinerate her knotted insides and blow them out with the smoke. Maybe then she would stop hurting.

Stop being a drama queen, Tara scolded herself. She picked up her phone again and scrolled through her contacts list. For a few seconds she stared at the number she had searched for. Then she got up and headed into the ladies', where she locked herself in a stall. She took a deep breath and pressed the dial icon.

"Hello?" It was the clipped, impersonal tone of someone who had answered their phone automatically, without looking at the caller's name.

Tara's throat was dry and she found herself unable to speak.

"Hello?" Milind's voice said again.

"Er, hi, Milind." Tara paused. "It's Tara."

This time the silence was from Milind's end. "Oh. Um, hi. What do you want?"

He didn't say it unkindly, but it cut Tara to the core. She swallowed, trying to get her heart down to where it belonged. "I...er... Sorry, is this a bad time?"

"Hang on." Some shuffling and muted voices came from the background. There was a creak, probably a door shutting, and then silence. Finally, Milind spoke again. "Yeah."

Tara cleared her throat. "I've, er, been calling...trying to get in touch with Sameen, but she's not been... I haven't been able to speak to her. Just wanted to check she's okay."

"Why?" Milind asked.

"Pardon?"

"Why are you trying to get in touch with Sameen?"

"Oh. I-I wanted to speak to her."

"Tara, isn't it clear she doesn't want to speak to you?"

"Yes, but—"

"I thought she told you that she doesn't want to have anything to do with you."

"I just need to talk to her...to explain."

"Explain what?"

"That…" Tara squeezed her eyes shut, struggling to find the right words. "I never knew," her voice was almost a whisper, "that she had feelings for me too."

"You would have known if you'd had the decen—" Milind stopped and sighed. "If you hadn't pulled away."

She leaned back against the bathroom door. "I should have never done that. I was wrong, Milind. Please, I need to talk to her, just once."

"I can give her a message," Milind said, "but I can't guarantee she'll speak to you."

"Please, can't you ask her to call me? I know she'll listen to you."

"Tara, I…" Milind exhaled loudly. "Listen, it's all very well for me to tell her to call you, but give me one good reason why she should. Tell me why, after you've hurt her, after you left her in the lurch, and weren't there when she really needed you."

Tara's throat hurt with the size of the lump lodged in it. "Because I love her too."

"That's not enough," said Milind. "At least it's not enough for you to say it. If you really loved her, you wouldn't have abandoned her or shut her out like you did. Actually, Tara, I'm sorry, but I can't pass on your message. I don't want to play any part in you putting my friend through the wringer. I don't want to see her hurt in this way again. I'm afraid I don't see any reason she should talk to you. Nothing in your actions over the past weeks convinces me that you are deserving of Sameen. If you want to contact her, you won't be doing it through me. I have to go now. Take care."

Tara heard a beep and then there was silence.

Chapter 27

"MY HOUSE IS GOING TO feel so empty," Sameen heard her mother telling Milind. "In a few days Danish will be leaving too, and then Sameen."

Sameen followed her voice out into the hall, where Milind was kneeling to put on his shoes. His luggage was lying next to him.

"I'm going to miss you all too, Aunty," he said. "Thank you so much for having me."

"Don't be silly," Sameen's mother responded. "You're welcome here anytime, you know that."

As he straightened, Sameen's mother pulled him into a hug. "Take care of yourself. And Sameen. Have you…spoken to your parents?"

She said the word "spoken" with a slight hesitation. Everyone knew it was a euphemism for much more complicated things.

Milind gave her a crooked smile. "I have." He waved a hand, as if to say it was all fine. He checked his phone. "My cab's almost here."

"Amma, Revathi-akka is calling you," Sameen said. She shook her head at her mother's retreating back. "Is it my imagination or is she getting a little deaf?"

"Your imagination," said Milind. "Listen, so what are your plans?"

Sameen pursed her lips. "I am going to miss you," she said, purposely avoiding his question. "I wish you didn't have to go."

"Those planes won't fly themselves. And looks like your employers are a lot more generous than mine. Extended leave." He snorted. "Whoever heard of such a thing?"

"Lucky me."

"Well, I'm going to miss you too." Milind put his arm around Sameen and squeezed. "You *are* going to come back to Delhi, right?"

"Of course I am. What kind of question is that?"

"It's just… I know things are difficult right now."

"I'm coming back," Sameen said firmly. "I just need a bit of time, you know, to sort myself out."

"I think Danish's idea is a good one—that you go with him to Singapore. A little bit of distance is great for clearing your head." He dropped his voice. "And mending your heart."

Sameen nodded. "Yeah, well, Danish thinks I'm stressed out because of my job."

"Doesn't matter why he thinks you're stressed out. Think about it, okay? I'd much rather have you back in Delhi right away, but I also want you to stop hurting."

A car pulled up outside the gates—Milind's taxi. Sameen's mother came out again, and there was another round of hugs. Sameen went back into the house, an air of melancholy descending around her. She found herself wandering towards the kitchen, where Revathi-akka was stirring something on the burner.

"Hey, Revathi-akka," Sameen said in English, "what's cooking?"

"Very brilliant cooking," Revathi-akka replied. She had an enviable English vocabulary, but a complete inability to put the words together in anything resembling syntax. "Most delicious experience. Very surprise. You waiting."

Sameen laughed. From the aroma of spices, she knew it was chicken curry.

"Are you staying for a while?" Revathi-akka switched to Kannada. She ladled a leg of chicken and some curry into a stainless-steel bowl and handed it to Sameen. "Your mother and father will be happy. It's nice to have you both here. Otherwise just us old people rattling around the house."

Sameen dipped her fingers into the curry, broke off a bit of chicken, and popped it into her mouth. "Mm. Amazing."

"More chilli?"

"No, it's perfect."

"Good." Revathi-akka turned off the burner and put a lid on the pan. At the same time the rice cooker switched itself off with a loud click.

"Wow, perfect timing."

Sameen sat on a stool in the corner of the kitchen and watched their old cook grate a cucumber into the curd. Then she took a small pan and set it on the other burner.

"You look sad," Revathi-akka said as she heated some oil and then added mustard seeds, curry leaves, and a few other odds and ends to the little pan. As they sputtered, filling the air with a familiar smell, she lifted the pan and upended its contents into the curd. There was an angry hiss as hot and cold came together. "Are you not happy in Delhi?"

"I am happy." *Kind of. At least, I was.*

"Your amma said there's a boy. Is he making you unhappy?"

"I think," Sameen said, her words measured, because she didn't want to lie to the woman who had been their nanny when she and Danish had been small, "I am the one making him unhappy."

"Happiness is a fickle friend, Baby." Revathi-akka reverted to the old childhood nickname, one that had caused many tears and recriminations after Milind had discovered it, told their other friends, and they had, in turn, tormented Sameen. "What makes you happy today may mean nothing tomorrow."

"So what are you saying? That one can never be happy?"

The cook shook her head as she poured chicken curry out into a serving dish. "All I'm saying is that there's no right or wrong sometimes."

Sameen stared at the little bowl in her hands. "If I go with Danish to Singapore, do you think I'd be running away?"

Revathi-akka's hands stilled. She turned, her eyes wide in surprise. "To live?"

"No, no," Sameen hastened to clarify. "Just for a little bit. To-to find out how I can be happy again."

The old woman smiled. "I think that would be a very good idea."

Tara looped her headphones around the back of her neck and reached into her pocket for her key. She had just inserted it into the lock when the door opened by itself. Her mother stared at her, puzzled.

"It's six in the morning," she said.

"I know," said Tara.

Her mother didn't respond, just continued to stare.

"Are you going to let me in, Mama?"

Her mother stood aside, still gazing at Tara like she was a ghost. "What are you doing up at six o'clock?"

"I went for a run." Tara plonked down on a stool and started to take off her running shoes. "It's nice outside at this time. No traffic."

"Yes, *I* know that. But I didn't think you even knew that six a.m. existed."

"Ha ha, funny." Tara rolled her eyes. "I'm going to make scrambled eggs. Okay with you?"

"Are you ill?" her mother asked.

"What?"

"Getting up early, going for a run, offering to make breakfast. It's like a Tara from a different universe."

"Mama, you've got to stop watching *Doctor Who*," Tara said, exasperated. "And just because you've been going for a yoga class at dawn for two days doesn't mean you get to be all high and mighty about getting up early."

"Hmm," her mother said. "I shall have two slices of toast with my eggs, and some fruit, please. Black tea."

"Oh Mama, I know. I make your breakfast almost every day."

She went to her room, shaking her head. Laugh at her mother or scream at her? Sometimes it was impossible to pick one. She stripped off her sweaty clothes and sat at the edge of her bed. Resuming her early-morning runs—well, it was more walking, to be honest—had felt good. She felt good, full of energy, positive, optimistic.

The new me.

If only she could stop her heart from racing with part dread and part anticipation.

She almost made it to the shower, but faltered at the last step.

Out of habit that was fast starting to get obsessive, her glance fell to her phone, lying face down on her table, tucked purposely behind the computer monitor.

Her pulse was pounding now, and her sense of anticipation had given her a dull pain just under her ribcage. She reached for the phone and pressed the power button. And the world crashed around her.

No unread messages, no missed calls, no emails. No Sameen.

Tara went into the bathroom and turned on the shower. As the hot water poured around her shoulders, she leaned her face up against the cascade.

I won't cry.

It was easy to tell herself it was just water and not tears rolling down her cheeks. Tara wiped them away angrily. She had no time for tears. If there was one thing she had decided, it was this: she was not giving up. Not this time. Because Barkha was right and Milind was right. If she wanted Sameen, she had to let Sameen choose her. And for that to happen, she had to be worth choosing.

She had no guarantee Sameen would forgive her, but Tara couldn't live the rest of her life knowing she had never tried.

I was so full of bullshit before.

The thought came to her like a sledgehammer, devastating in its directness.

It was true. The past few weeks had shown her that she wanted nothing more than to be with Sameen. Yes, she knew *having* Sameen was not so black and white as Tara making up her mind to woo her back. But she needed to do this for herself—to prove to herself that even if Sameen was lost to her forever, she was someone who would have been worthy anyway.

As for the world, the world be damned.

She didn't have to have a big coming-out drama. This was her life and her reality, not one of the foreign TV series she watched that seemed to exist in alien worlds. What she needed, what she had always needed but had been too stupid to see—even though Barkha had—was to live her life on her own terms. That didn't need any big announcements, only the courage to be honest with herself.

Chapter 28

SAMEEN PUSHED OPEN THE DOOR that led to Stone Apple's offices and breathed in the familiar slightly damp smell masked by a flowery one. Everything looked exactly the same as when she'd left on her holiday more than a month ago. The pristine white sitting area, the ceiling-high bookshelves stacked neatly with all the books that the publishing house had produced in its life, the reception desk, and the woman sitting behind it, Aditi, who was currently talking on the phone in her most professional voice but still grinned broadly when Sameen walked in. All of it gave Sameen a sense of belonging and reminded her why she had chosen to come back. She loved her job, and the people she worked with weren't too bad either.

"You're back!" Aditi cried after hanging up the phone.

"Hi, Aditi." Sameen grinned. She really liked this perpetually cheerful woman.

"How was Singapore? I've heard it's very pretty."

"Yes, it is. And very organized."

The holiday had been exactly what Sameen had needed to distance herself from the situation and clear her head. She had finally come to accept that Tara would and could no longer be a part of her life. That however much she loved Tara and yearned for her, and how the thought of not seeing her broke every bit of Sameen's heart to pieces, she had to find a way of putting Tara behind her. That was the only way she could continue living, even though without Tara it would be half a life. But she had come back from Singapore rejuvenated, more in control of her feelings, and more confident about taking on the world.

"How are things here?" she asked Aditi.

"Baani broke her arm—she was jumping a red light and got hit by another scooter. Chaturvedi-ji had a baby girl and is super excited about it—he brought in the most delicious laddoos I've had in my life. And Loveleen Bing came in yesterday to meet Jugal, asked to see the sales figures of her book for the last three months. She almost drove him to tears analysing and questioning every sale."

Aditi was a big gossip, but that was probably a part of every receptionist's job.

"Oh dear," Sameen said. "Poor Baani and Jugal. But I'm really glad for Chaturvedi-ji. He's been desperate for a girl for such a long time. I'll talk to them as soon as I'm settled in. Were there any messages for me while I was away?"

"Just a couple from Ms Bing. She's found a new cover designer for the next book. And the boss wants to meet you at two p.m."

Sameen sighed inwardly. Loveleen hadn't even finished writing her first draft yet, which was going to take at least a year to see the light of day, and she was already planning the cover design. Such a control freak.

"Okay, thanks, Aditi. I'll catch up with you and the gang at lunch."

Sameen walked towards her office. The feeling of coming home was reinforced when she entered her room. Everything was exactly how she'd left it and just how she liked it—messy and disorganized. She was never apologetic about her mess because there was a method to it, and it never hampered her efficiency.

She sat at her desk, booted her computer, and picked up the coffee mug that the office assistant had placed before her. She sipped the hot beverage as she scrolled down her inbox, running her eyes over the unread emails. Her finger stopped mid-scroll as she caught the name of the sender of two of the messages.

Tara.

Sameen released a slow breath to calm her nerves. Soon after their meeting in Matteo, Sameen had blocked Tara's email address as well as her phone number. But two emails somehow seemed to have sneaked into Sameen's inbox.

She debated whether to open them. Was it a good idea? What if it brought back a new wave of pain that took her back to square one?

Let me at least check why they didn't get automatically deleted.

She clicked on the older of the two messages and glanced at the header. Tara had sent it from a different email address, which was how it had managed to bypass the filter Sameen had set up.

Unable to help herself, she let her eyes be drawn to the body of the email.

5 February
Sameen,

I wish I could say it better than Luke did, but I can't. So I'll let him say it again. But know this—I mean every word with all my heart.

Sameen clicked on the video embedded under the message. It was her favourite scene from *Gilmore Girls*. Luke and Lorelai on their first date, and Luke telling Lorelai, "Lorelai, this thing we're doing here—me, you—I just want you to know I'm in, I'm all in."

Something took hold of Sameen's heart and squeezed. Before she could dwell on the feeling, she clicked on other email.

10 February
Sameen,

I have sent several emails to you in the past few months, but your silence indicates that in your eyes I'm beyond redemption. Who can blame you? My mistakes have been great, and even if you somehow found it in your generous heart to forgive me, I won't be able to forgive myself. Your silence and your desire to not communicate with me have been unbearable, but they are what I deserve.

Writing to you has been like a lifeline for me; the only air I have been able to breathe. Though I don't think you have read any of them, these emails have made me feel connected to you. But I think it is time for me to not be selfish and stop harassing you like this. I'm going to respect your wishes to leave you alone, but please don't think I am giving up on you. I could never do that. Ever.

I will endure my punishment in silence and I will wait for you. I hope that some day you will be able to pick up the phone and dial my number.

Until we meet again.

Yours,
Tara

Tears were streaming down Sameen's face by the time she finished reading the email. She wished she could actually do what Tara had asked her to: pick up the phone and call her. But that was no longer an option. It was too late. Too much had happened and there was too much hurt. Sameen had no idea how to let go of the resentment she had for Tara, and to forgive her for betraying their friendship.

She got up and stumbled into the bathroom. She leaned over the sink, helpless against the heaving sobs that wrenched her into pieces. Finally, when the tears were all out, Sameen washed her face, took a deep breath, and readied herself to face the world again.

When she stepped back into her office, Aditi walked in with a package in her hand, which she placed on Sameen's desk.

"I forgot to give this to you earlier. It came a few weeks ago."

"Thanks," Sameen said, silently thanking her stars that Aditi hadn't walked in earlier when she had been a crying mess. She turned her face away, pretending to study the package, so the other woman wouldn't see her red eyes.

It was a rectangular box wrapped in brown paper and tied with a string. *Books I guess*, Sameen said to herself as she sat on her chair, pulled the box to her lap, and loosened the string.

But the box didn't contain books. It had Tara's *Casablanca* puzzle, with a note:

7 February

Sameen,

Without you I'm just a bundle of mismatched pieces that don't make sense. Without you I'm incomplete.

Tara

Sameen couldn't help the tears from falling again. She wished she could find a way back to Tara, but from where she was standing, it looked impossible.

One thing was clear to her now, though—it was time to call Rohan.

Tara waited for the boarding announcement for her flight back to Delhi. Getting back home would be a relief. She was exhausted. Her two-day stay in Ahmedabad had been a bit of a blur. She could barely even remember what had happened at the game she had been sent to cover.

These days, it was all she could do to keep moving and doing the things she was supposed to. Even sitting in an uncomfortable seat, waiting for her flight's turn to board. Any other time, Tara would have been reading a magazine and tapping her feet impatiently, wondering how much longer it would be. But she was numb now. It was as though she'd forgotten how to feel.

Keeping herself busy was her lifeline now. Because stopping meant being flooded with thoughts of Sameen, and that was somewhere Tara didn't want to go.

Sameen had been The One, and Tara had pushed her away. Finally and completely. Her silence proved that. Every minute, every hour, every day that passed since her last email to Sameen, was another nail in the coffin of what they could have had. Even though Tara had meant every word of what she'd said—that she was going to wait for Sameen—she'd had no idea how excruciating that would be. Worse was the knowledge that she'd had a chance with Sameen and blown it. Sameen had most likely gone back to Rohan. It was over.

Barkha had been right—she *was* a coward. At least, she had been.

How was she supposed to live without Sameen, never hearing her voice, and never seeing her laugh? But at least she knew now that Sameen had been right—their friendship could not be salvaged. In fact, it had stopped being a friendship a long time ago. It had been love. And now its only existence was a gnawing ache in Tara's heart.

She was nudged out of her rumination by a movement near the gates. The boarding announcement hadn't happened yet, but the ground staff were getting ready.

Then she saw why. The flight crew were heading towards the gate, the flight attendants in gaudy red and yellow, and the pilots in smart black and white. She inhaled sharply. Was that Milind?

She racked her brains, trying to recall which airline he worked for, as she looked down and away, hoping that if it was Milind, he wouldn't notice her. Thinking about the last time they'd spoken made her cringe; she still hadn't got over the shame she had felt at Milind's words.

"Tara?"

Damn. Did nothing go her way these days? Heart pounding, she looked up at him. And there he was, a hint of a smile on his face. Tara forced herself to look surprised and managed a smile back.

"Oh, Milind, hi."

"Hi. Are you on my flight?"

"Looks like it."

"So how are you?"

"I'm fine. And you?"

"I'm well too."

Someone from the crew called out to him.

"Listen, I have to get going," he said, "but can we talk? Will you meet me in Delhi after we land? There's that bar right outside the airport."

"Um...uh... I don't know..." The last thing Tara wanted was to spend time with him. The conversation would definitely veer towards Sameen, and she didn't know if she could handle hearing about her and Rohan.

"Please. It's important."

It was hard to refuse Milind's imploring look, and Tara had no energy to fight him. "Okay."

Three hours later, she was sitting in the bar, nursing a gin and tonic, when Milind arrived. He sat next to her on one of the tall stools.

"Boy, that was a tough flight. I really need a drink." He signalled to the bartender. "I'll have what she's having."

"So what important thing did you want to talk to me about?" Tara asked.

He gave her a curious look. "You don't believe in pleasantries, do you?"

Tara felt a little sheepish.

"Well, nothing much," he continued. "Just wanted to catch up with you. The last time we talked, it was a bit...you know. I hope there are no hard feelings."

Tara's smile was rueful. "That's okay. You don't need to explain yourself. I deserved every bit of it." And because she couldn't help herself, she asked, "How is...Sameen?"

"She got back from Singapore last week."

"She was in Singapore? Visiting her brother?"

"Yep."

With Rohan? But Tara couldn't bring herself to ask him that. An awkward silence ensued.

"So...what are you up to?" Milind asked her.

She shrugged. "The usual." She glanced at her drink, wishing she could drown herself in it.

"Tara, are you really okay?"

She sighed. "I'm trying."

This time the silence was so long that Tara had to look up to check if Milind was still there or if he'd legged it. He was, and he was staring at her. Even in the dim lighting of the bar, she could tell his eyes were narrowed like he was considering something serious. She was starting to get a little tired of people staring at her contemplatively these days.

Finally, he tore his eyes away, diverting his gaze into his drink. Then he looked up again. "Far be it from me to interfere, but there is something I think I should tell you."

Chapter 29

SAMEEN SWITCHED ON THE KETTLE and watched as tiny bubbles formed in the water. It was a Friday evening, and the thought of the weekend scared her. Outside, it was pouring with rain.

When her tea was done, she took it over to the dining table where the jigsaw pieces were spread out. A corner of the movie poster of *Casablanca* was beginning to take shape. Sameen's eyes blurred with tears.

She had thought that she had come back from her three weeks in Singapore all sorted, and firm in her resolve to forget about Tara and get on with her life. But those last two emails from her and then the puzzle had smashed that resolve to smithereens.

If this was how much keeping her distance was going to hurt, Sameen didn't know how she was going to survive it. She didn't know it was possible to feel this much pain without being physically injured.

She wiped her eyes with the back of her hand and looked at the puzzle again. She reached out and fitted two pieces together, part of Ingrid Bergman. Her eyes filled with tears again.

"Okay. That's it." She slapped her hands on the table and stood up. She brushed her tears away again.

She slipped on her shoes, picked up her keys and umbrella, and was out of the house in less than half a minute.

She half walked, half ran down the lane, dodging the puddles, taking all the shortcuts that had become so familiar over the past months. She kept her head down against the driving rain, thankful that having to concentrate on finding a dry path through the puddle-filled potholes was keeping her from thinking about what she had set out to do.

But when she reached the gate, unlatched it, crossed the courtyard, and reached for the doorbell, she noticed the big lock on the door.

Sameen's legs were suddenly jelly. She sat down heavily on the stairs. The adrenaline rush drained away, leaving her spent.

What was I thinking anyway?

The walk back took much longer even though the rain had eased to a steady drizzle. She climbed the stairs to her flat listlessly, the thought of going back in there almost too unbearable.

She climbed the last few steps and was reaching for the light switch on the landing when a movement caught her eye.

Tara was sitting on the floor with her back against the door. She was completely drenched and had a small travel bag by her side.

For a few seconds, Sameen gaped at her visitor, who unfolded herself and stood. She was shivering.

"Y-you're soaked," was all Sameen managed when she finally spoke.

"Yes." Tara looked down at herself, like she hadn't noticed it.

"You should get warm," Sameen said. Yet she found herself immobile. She felt like she had fallen down a rabbit hole. Not ten minutes ago she had run to Tara's house to…to do what exactly? And now Tara was standing at her door.

Was it a sign of some sort? Or was she actually dreaming?

"I suppose I should," Tara replied.

That roused Sameen out of her daze. "Um, what?"

"What you said, that I should get warm."

"Oh, of course." Sameen fumbled for her key. "Come in, I'll get you some clothes." She unlocked the door and led Tara in. "You know where the towels are?"

Tara nodded. She slipped off her shoes and walked towards the bathroom. She waited, dripping on the floor mat, shivering, until Sameen got her some clothes.

Still in a state of disbelief, Sameen mopped up the trail of water Tara had left across the house while Tara changed in the bathroom. Sameen then went back into the kitchen and made them both a cup of tea. Her head was buzzing with questions. What was Tara doing here? What did she want?

Sameen carried the mugs into the living room and placed them on the dining table, as Tara appeared at the door, now dry and apparently warm.

"I made some tea." Sameen pointed towards the mugs.

"Thanks." Tara picked one up, and came and stood next to Sameen. The proximity made Sameen's heart race. The urge to touch her was almost irresistible. Despite her bemusement over Tara's sudden appearance at her doorstep, it was all she could do not to turn towards her and close the distance between them.

"So you're working on it again?" Tara asked.

"I wanted to see if I could finish it."

Sameen watched as Tara picked up a piece of Ingrid Bergman's hat and slid it into its place in the puzzle. Sameen followed suit with another one that filled the hole in her shoulder. A few more puzzle pieces found their home in silence.

"Are you going to tell me why you're here?" Sameen asked finally.

"Why didn't you tell me?"

"Tell you what?"

"About Rohan."

"How did you find out?"

"I bumped into Milind at the airport today."

Sameen sipped from her mug without replying.

"So why didn't you tell me that you broke up with Rohan?" Tara asked again. "You told me you were working things out with him."

Sameen found she couldn't focus on the jigsaw anymore. She moved to sit on the sofa and placed her mug on the coffee table.

"I think you misunderstood. What I meant was that it was becoming clear to me that I could no longer be with him."

"Why not?"

"Because it wouldn't be fair either to him or me to pretend I still loved him."

She glanced towards Tara, who was still near the table, fingering one of the jigsaw pieces. From her expression, it was clear she had no interest in the puzzle.

"But what I don't understand," Sameen said, "is what changed for you. You clearly said you didn't want a relationship. So I spent the better part of last month trying to come to terms with a life that didn't have you in it. And then I came back and saw the emails and everything else you had been sending me. What do you want, Tara? Why are you messing with my head?"

Tara put the jigsaw piece in her hand back on the table and stared at it for a few seconds. Then she started to talk, hesitantly at first, and then with more and more confidence.

"For a long time, I thought I could control my emotions, not fall in love if I didn't want to, and push all attraction aside. After many years of living like that, I had even managed to convince myself that I was in charge. Then you came along and everything changed. I don't know when and I don't know how. I tried so hard and so many times to stamp out my feelings, but everything I did only fanned the fire, and each time it grew bigger and more powerful. Before I knew it, I had fallen deeply, madly in love with you. It terrified me. That's when I ran."

Tara laughed mirthlessly. "So imagine my shock when I realized there was no place I could go to get away from you, from my feelings for you. They were with me everywhere, following me around like a shadow. I couldn't take one step without you. I couldn't breathe. How did I ever think I could forget you? That I could live without you?" Her eyes filled with tears.

"When you told me you loved me, that's when I knew what an idiot I'd been. I'd singlehandedly destroyed the one thing that is most precious to me in the entire world. I thought I'd lost you forever when you refused to take my calls or answer my emails. But after I met Milind today and he told me about Rohan, I knew I had to come talk to you.

"I've wasted so much time, Sameen. Time we could've had together if it hadn't been for my pig-headedness. I don't want to do that anymore. Not for one more second."

She moved towards Sameen and sat next to her, taking her hands. Sameen didn't move. She couldn't have even if she'd wanted to.

"Will you please forgive me? Will you let me back in your life?"

Sameen stared at Tara, unable to stop her own tears from spilling out. She wiped her nose with the back of her hand.

"Do you know where I've just been?" she asked.

Tara looked at her quizzically.

"To your house," Sameen replied. "I went there to talk to you. When I saw the lock on the door, I thought it was a sign or something. I came back home, and there you were, sitting on my doorstep like a drowned rat."

Tara uttered what sounded like a chuckle, but Sameen could see the apprehension on her face. Sameen looked down at their joined hands.

"Will you promise me something?" she asked.

"Anything."

"Promise me that the next time you run, you'll take me with you."

Tara's eyes filled with tears again, but this time Sameen knew they were no longer sad.

"I promise."

Tara leaned forward and her lips brushed against Sameen's. A warmth spread through Sameen's body. She reached for Tara, one hand weaving through the back of Tara's hair, the other curling around Tara's neck, pulling her closer. There was a pounding in her ears—she couldn't tell if that was her own heart or Tara's.

It started off as a gentle kiss, and then it was as though the floodwaters had broken through, unleashing the pent-up emotions of the past weeks. They kissed with an urgency, the crush of their bodies and the frenzy of their mouths making it seem as if this moment was all they had. To Sameen it felt like a gift, one that she had never thought she could have, but now that she did, she knew she could never have enough. Her world was tumbling forward head over heels and she felt wonderful.

They were both breathing hard when they broke apart. Sameen opened her eyes to catch a glimpse of Tara's long eyelashes that tickled her own. Tara opened her eyes and let their foreheads touch.

"I've been wanting to kiss you again since the New Year's party," Sameen said softly as she caressed the side of Tara's mouth with her thumb.

"You know how long I've been wanting to kiss you?"

"Hmm?"

"Since the evening of the book launch."

"No. Really?"

"Yep."

"We have a lot of catching up to do then." Sameen moved her lips to Tara's again, then stopped abruptly.

"Aren't you going to call your mother?" she asked.

"Huh? What?"

"Don't you think you should let her know you won't be coming home tonight?"

"Sounds like a very good idea." Tara's tone was teasing. "But you should know that this means I'll have to get up from this sofa, fish out the phone from my bag, dial her number, and answer her many questions before she lets me go."

Tara made to get up, but Sameen pulled her back. "Maybe later."

This is the first day of the rest of my life. The thought floated into Tara's head as she watched the edge of the sky starting to turn a lighter grey. *The first day. Of the rest of my life.*

She repeated the words to herself. As trite as they sounded, there was a ring of truth to them. Tara had chosen happiness. Finally. It settled around her shoulders like a whisper, like a delicate shawl so soft that it felt weightless against her body, yet it wrapped her in a warmth that seeped into her bones and made her feel safe.

But "happiness" was such an inadequate term. It had a certain sharpness to it, an edge, a coarseness. Happy was about being pleased, like when she wrote an incisive match report. An evening out with friends could make her happy. She could be happy about getting a good deal on Amazon.

What she felt having Sameen next to her, knowing she could reach out and touch her, aware they could have the rest of their lives together, was a very different feeling altogether. It was deep and soft and subtle. It filled her senses and it filled her physical body. It made her feel invincible.

"Contentment". Maybe that described it a whole lot better.

Or maybe there wasn't a word for it.

Tara pulled her arms out from under the quilt and folded them under her head. She shifted slightly to get a better view of Sameen, fast asleep, the quilt pulled up almost to her nose, rising and falling as she breathed, her frizzy hair fanned out on the pillow.

It was cold—winter was being kind to them this year, having decided to stay a bit longer than usual—and Tara's arms were covered in goosebumps in seconds. But she didn't mind. She was a Delhi girl—she liked the cold; she could handle it.

She turned on her side and draped her arm lightly over Sameen. Despite her best efforts to be gentle, Sameen stirred.

She opened her eyes and smiled sleepily. "Hey."

"Hey yourself."

"Sleep well?"

Tara propped herself up on an elbow. "I'm not sure. A certain someone kept me awake most of the night." She smiled down at Sameen and reached up to brush the hair away from her face.

"Really, now, who might that be?" Sameen said, her voice low. She closed her eyes at Tara's touch.

"It's all a bit of a blur. I'm not sure I remember much."

Sameen popped open one eye. "Would you like some help jogging your memory?"

"Yes, I think I'll take you up on that offer," Tara murmured.

Sameen's mouth twitched. "I like this new you."

"You do, do you? Why is that?"

"Because it's good to see that you've embraced your lesbosity back wholeheartedly."

Tara laughed. "And you seem to have accepted yours with admirable equanimity."

"Were you expecting me to have a crisis?"

"Mm, I think I'm managing fine without it," Tara said, placing a finger on Sameen's lips. "But, I'm sorry to tell you, Ms Hotshot Editor, 'lesbosity' is not a real word."

"Isn't English an evolving language?"

"You would prefer a discussion on semantics?"

"No thank you," Sameen said, her tone contrite, a smile still edging her words. "There are other things I'd rather do."

Tara's voice was a whisper. "Such as?"

"I'd rather not say," Sameen went on, her voice even softer now, sending currents of anticipation down Tara's body, "because there's this adage we editors rather like, and that is, 'show, don't tell'."

That left Tara incapable of further intellectual exchange. They lay facing each other, separated only by a whisper of air. Sameen ran a hand along the edges of Tara's face and came to rest on the side of her neck. Her fingers were warm against Tara's chilled face. She closed her eyes as Sameen's lips met hers.

Epilogue

"OH MAMA, WILL YOU PLEASE stop stressing?" Tara ran her fingers through her hair in frustration. "Your taxi is waiting. You have nine old ladies waiting to be taken to McLeod Ganj. Just go."

"Make sure you water my plants daily. Just because you won't be living here anymore doesn't mean you don't have a responsibility to this house."

"Don't worry, Chhaya. I will wake her up early every day to come water the plants," Sameen said with a mischievous glint in her eyes.

Tara glared at her threateningly.

"My only child going away to live somewhere else," said Chhaya with a dramatic sigh, a hand on her chest.

Tara rolled her eyes. "Mama, stop it! Ever since you started taking these women on tours all over the country, you're the one who has hardly been home. So if anyone should complain, it should be me. Also, I'm not moving to the other side of the world. I'm only moving upstairs, for heaven's sake."

Sameen had been looking for a new place to get away from the house she had set up with Rohan. So when Chhaya's first-floor tenants had moved out earlier in the year, she'd moved upstairs. For a while, the arrangement worked fine, but now, ten months later, considering Tara spent most of her time upstairs anyway, they had decided that she should move in with Sameen. It made little difference as Tara would also stay close to her mother—always a good idea in case she took on any more extreme hobbies.

"Chhaya, don't you trust me to take good care of her?" Sameen asked, making puppy-dog eyes at her.

Tara knew that look very well. It had the power to move mountains and melt rocks. She had been at the receiving end of it many times in the past year that she and Sameen had been together. And she knew that, with that look, whatever Sameen wanted, Sameen got.

"The only reason I'm letting her move out is because she's going to live with you, Sameen," Chhaya said. "If it were anybody else, there's no way they'd have been able to take her away from me."

"Oh my god," said Tara, rolling her eyes again. "Sometimes it seems like you two are stuck in a Bollywood film."

Sameen ignored the jibe. "Then go on your trip and leave your house and your daughter to me," she said. It was no less dramatic. "Rest assured that when you come back, everything will be just the same and we will be here waiting for you."

Chhaya sighed. "Yes, of course. Okay, I'll be going, then."

She hugged Sameen and then Tara. She got into the cab and waved until it turned the corner.

"Phew!" Tara plonked herself down on the sofa, while Sameen shut the door. "She's so exhausting."

"Nah, she's cool."

"Right," said Tara, rubbing her hands. "Let's pack some boxes and get this show on the road. Even if the road is just two flights of stairs."

She started to get up, but Sameen pushed her back on the sofa, kneeling by her and running her finger down Tara's arm. "Or," she said slowly, "we could leave the boxes for a little bit and find other ways of exercising our limbs."

"Are you propositioning me, Ms Siddiqi?" Tara enquired with one eyebrow raised, her gaze following the movement of the finger.

"Why yes, I certainly am, Ms Dixit. How did you know?"

"Just a wild guess," Tara replied as Sameen pushed her down and straddled her thighs. Tara's fingers brushed against Sameen's cheeks, sliding into her hair as she pulled Sameen's face down towards her.

But before their lips could meet, there was a knock on the door. Sameen groaned and said something colourful in Punjabi that even Tara, who had grown up in Delhi, had never dared to voice.

"I'll get it," she added. "It must be Barkha with the cartons she promised." She fixed her hair and opened the door.

"Hi, Sameen." Barkha swept in, followed by Kunal staggering under the weight of an armful of flat-packed cardboard cartons. She stopped short of the sofa and gave Tara a once-over. "Oh, look at my baby. All grown up and finally moving out to live with her girlfriend. I never thought this day would come."

"Hello to you too," Tara said. "And once again, I'm only moving *upstairs*!"

"Er, where should I put these?" Kunal asked.

"Follow me." Sameen led him down the corridor towards Tara's room.

"He-ey," a new voice called out. "Anyone hungry?"

It was Ashish, with Milind, each of them carrying bags from which delicious smells wafted.

"Oh good, the food is here." Tara grabbed a packet from Milind and headed for the kitchen. Ashish followed to help as they laid out samosas, dhokla, and lemonade, while the others chatted and assembled cartons.

After a short break for snacks, they got down to business. Between them, they were going to lug Tara's furniture up, while they would pack the rest of her stuff in boxes and suitcases. Milind had brought along a marker that he used liberally on the boxes—"It's very easy to mix them up," he said. "I should know, I've moved a lot."

A couple of hours later, Tara's room was rather bare. She couldn't help feeling a little tug at the thought of moving out. She had spent almost all her life in this house. When she had been five, her mother had read her the entire set of Noddy books over one weekend, curled up on the carpet in the living room. She was eight when she'd hidden her first secret journal, taped behind the cistern in the bathroom, which had turned into a soggy mess eventually. This was where she had agonized over her first crush (maths teacher in class three), sitting at her desk, and making cards she'd never given her. This was the same bed in the same room where she and Radhika had first had sex. And it was the bed she'd fallen into and cried when they'd broken up. This was the hall where she and her father had played cricket with a ping-pong ball and a rolled-up newspaper on Sundays. She remembered watching *Grey's Anatomy* on the living room TV three years ago when the phone call about her father had come.

"Tara, what about your latest jigsaw puzzle?" Barkha called out, yanking her out of her trip down memory lane.

Tara blinked. Her eyes were moist. She wasn't moving away, she reminded herself, and she would be here almost every day. "Er, let it be," she called out.

Sameen's arm slipped around her. "What's the matter?" she said. "Having second thoughts?"

Tara smiled and leaned into Sameen. "No. Just thinking about all the memories I have here."

"We'll make new ones."

"I know," she said, giving Sameen a quick peck on the lips.

Hand in hand, they went out into the living room where Milind and Kunal were organizing the boxes. Ashish was bent over the half-finished 500-piece puzzle of a garden on the coffee table. He looked up apologetically at Tara. "Sorry, I saw a piece that fit."

"It's fine," said Tara, giving Sameen's hand a squeeze. "Sometimes the pieces just fall into place."

About Sheryn Munir

Sheryn Munir is a big fan of romances. After reading countless lesbian romance novels based in Western countries, she desperately wanted to read one based in India. Realising that she'd have to wait forever for that wish to come true, she decided to have a crack at writing one herself. *Falling into Place* is the result of that endeavour.

Sheryn was born in Lucknow and grew up in Delhi, India. Though she started writing from the age of seven, she was only recently inspired to write an entire book in a genre close to her heart that is about her own people. Sheryn has studied journalism and freelances as a writer, editor, and web developer. While she likes visiting new places, the journeys are a tad unpleasant. She has a weakness for chocolates, Indian street foods, and British television dramas. She lives in Delhi with three laptops and an e-reader.

CONNECT WITH SHERYN
Website: www.sherynmunir.com
Twitter: twitter.com/sherynmunir

Other Books from Ylva Publishing

www.ylva-publishing.com

Where the Light Plays

C. Fonseca

ISBN: 978-3-95533-421-5
Length: 285 pages (97,000 words)

Dr. Caitlin Quinn is a sophisticated, self-assured Irish art historian visiting Australia on sabbatical. That doesn't mean she can't enjoy the local scenery—especially sun-kissed Surf Coast artist Andi Rey. Their attraction is unstoppable, but their lives are moving in opposite directions. Andi doesn't need distractions, and a woman that eschews commitment spells trouble, with a capital "T".

Party Wall

Cheyenne Blue

ISBN: 978-3-95533-886-2
Length: 223 pages (63,000 words)

The moment Freya looks at the new sex shop, she knows it will clash with her new-age store next door. She's right. Outgoing newcomer Lily begins to intrude on Freya's ordered life. The woman stands for everything Freya has lost—playfulness, spontaneity—even sex. But does Lily have more in common with Freya than the wall that divides them? A lesbian romance about crossing lines that hold us back.

Falling into Place
© 2018 by Sheryn Munir

ISBN: 978-3-95533-972-2

Also available as e-book.

Published by Ylva Publishing, legal entity of Ylva Verlag, e.Kfr.

Ylva Verlag, e.Kfr.
Owner: Astrid Ohletz
Am Kirschgarten 2
65830 Kriftel
Germany

www.ylva-publishing.com

First edition: 2018

Credits
Edited by Lee Winter and JoSelle
Proofread by Amanda Jean
Cover Design and Print Layout by Streetlight Graphics

CPSIA information can be obtained
at www.ICGtesting.com
Printed in the USA
LVHW030023161221
706193LV00004B/66